AN AMISH THANKSGIVING BLESSING

AN AMISH ROMANCE

Naomi Troyer

Contents

Chapter 1
A Familye Legacy

Hannah folded her hands in her lap, feeling more alone than she had ever felt before. The room smelled like lemon furniture oil, and sunlight poured in through the large window. There was a big leather sofa beneath the window, the perfect spot for a late afternoon nap.

But she wasn't here to take a nap, she reminded herself. She was here to meet with Mr. Marlington. Her throat constricted with emotion as she remembered the events that had led to this meeting.

At twenty-three, Hannah Yoder had never contemplated losing her parents. At least not this early in life. She had envisioned a future where her children would grow up with a grossmammi and a grosspappi, only to lose her parents even before she found a man with whom she wanted to build a family.

The door opened and a tall man walked into the office. He wore a dark grey suit, a crisp white shirt, and a pair of spectacles. His eyes seemed hard, but they softened as he took a seat behind the table.

"Good morning…. Miss Yoder?" Mr. Marlington said as he removed his glasses.

Hannah nodded. "Jah, please call me Hannah."

"Very well Hannah. Before we begin, I just want to say I am very sorry for your loss." Mr. Marlington paused for a moment, as if a few brief seconds were enough for Hannah to get over the grief of losing her parents.

When her parents had told her they were travelling cross-country to visit her aunt in California, Hannah had been excited about the adventure they were about to undertake. Never in a million years had she expected both of her parents to lose their lives in a raging wildfire.

Her aunt had phoned, devastated, to relay the news. It had been an accident. No one had been at fault except for the raging flames that devoured their buggy with them inside. Her parents had gone to town and took a detour on the way back to her aunt's community. Unfortunately, that same day a wildfire had raged through the neighboring county, an hour's drive north.

The fire had surrounded them before they even realized what was happening. Regardless of the firefighters and rescue attempts to save their lives, the fire had been too fast, too furious.

Hannah had barely slept through the night since the news of her parents' demise. Nightmares haunted her dreams.

"The reason I asked you to meet me today is to discuss your father's will," the lawyer explained, drawing Hannah's attention back to him.

Hannah nodded. The bishop had explained to her as much.

"Your father was a humble man and I'm glad to inform you he had no debts. As wonderful as that might be, his only asset is the farm you are currently living on." Mr. Marlington paused again.

Hannah waited for him to continue, wishing he would just get to the point he was trying to make. She had a lot of work waiting for her on the farm. Although her father had sowed some pumpkin seed before the accident claimed his life, Hannah still had more than half the farm to sow.

As pumpkin farmers, the Yoders only had a few months every year to sow, grow, and harvest enough pumpkins to provide them with a cash income to last them the rest of the year. Although they were mostly subsistence farmers, there were a lot of things you still had to pay for. Fuel, gas, certain pantry items, and quite a few other things you needed to buy with cash.

"I'm sure you are aware of the balance of your father's savings account? It isn't much. I'm uncertain a young lady like yourself could survive on it for very long. It's for that reason that I've come up with a solution that will make your life much more comfortable and the work much less."

"What solution?" Hannah asked curiously. "If you're going to suggest I take out a loan to hire a farm manager, you're wrong. Daed insisted farm managers only work for their salary, no one farms the land like a farmer who owns it."

"Are you a farmer, Hannah?" Mr. Marlington asked with a cocked brow. "Because from what I can tell, your entire income relies on your yearly pumpkin harvest. If you can't farm pumpkins, you're going to end up losing the farm." Mr. Marlington sighed and shook his head. "I'm not trying to frighten you; I'm simply trying to give you the best possible advice."

"And what would that be?" Hannah asked stubbornly. She had just lost her parents; she wasn't about to lose her family farm as well.

"I've received a valuation on your farm. If you sell the farm, you wouldn't ever have to work another day in your life. You could buy a small cottage in the community and live comfortably for the rest of your life. I think it's what your father would've wanted."

Hannah frowned and shook her head. "What my daed would've wanted was for me to keep the familye land. That farm has been in our familye since 1794 when it was gifted to my great-great-great-great grosspappi for helping establish the community. How can you just expect me to sell it? Greed is a sin and no amount of money can replace a familye's legacy."

"I'm sorry if I offended you, Hannah, that wasn't my intention. I simply meant that running a pumpkin farm is a lot of work for a woman on her own. Of course, if you want to keep it, I'll have the deed transferred to your name," Mr. Marlington backed off.

Hannah nodded firmly. "Then that is what you'll do. Denke."

"But I must say this one last time. If you fall behind on your property taxes, you might lose the farm. With what little savings you have... that means one failed harvest and you'll lose your family legacy," Mr. Marlington pointed out.

Hannah stood up and crossed her arms defiantly. "I won't fail. You can send word when I need to sign anything, but if you'll excuse me, I have a pumpkin harvest to plan." Hannah walked out of Mr. Marlington's office feeling emotionally drained.

She knew she had just made the right decision by keeping the farm, but she couldn't help but fear that she would fail. She might have been raised on a pumpkin farm, but her father was the farmer.

Hannah knew a little about farming pumpkins, but she didn't know how her father grew his giant pumpkins or how he grew rows of pumpkins all the same size. She wasn't sure how often they were watered or how frequently they were weeded.

She stepped onto the sidewalk and saw the library across the road. Hannah had never been fond of reading, but she realized there and then that if she wanted to have a successful harvest, she was going to learn everything she could about pumpkins.

Starting with the different varieties.

Chapter 2
Opportunity Revealed

Joseph Slaber held his future in his hands.

Few people would understand how a farmer looked at seeds. Especially a pumpkin farmer looking at seeds that might just bring him the grand prize at the fall fair. Every year, he harvested some of his own seeds, but every year he bought seeds as well.

The combination gave him a good return with every harvest.

Although the Amish didn't celebrate Halloween like the Englisch culture did, for Joseph, Halloween was his best source of income—that and the fall fair. Not only did it give him the opportunity to sell the harvests of his hard work, but the opportunity to compete for the largest pumpkin of the year award.

He sowed the seeds in the tilled dirt, enjoying the warm summer air that brought him the scent of freshly dug earth. The soil was fertile this year, promising to deliver him one of his best years yet. As he walked through the dirt, dropping a seed every few feet, he remembered how he had walked these same fields with his father.

Joseph's mother had passed away giving birth to him, but Joseph had never felt disadvantaged for not having a mother, instead he had felt privileged to have a wonderful father. Since he could walk, Joseph had joined his father in the fields. He had worked alongside his father until his father's heart gave him trouble.

Little by little, Joseph took over the pumpkin farm and his father stepped back. When his father's heart finally failed and he was called home to the heavenly gates, Joseph had only been twenty-three years old. But with years of experience and learning from his father, Joseph had taken on his heritage without hesitation.

His only regret was losing the grand prize at the fair the year before. Eli Yoder had always been his father's greatest competition in growing the largest pumpkin. Every year their pumpkins only differed a few ounces. Some years, the Yoders would win the prize and other years, the Slabers would win the prize.

But over the last few years, Joseph's family had only brought the prize home once every three years. Eli Yoder had discovered the secret to growing prize pumpkins and Joseph had feared the fall festival this later this year. He knew his father would be proud of what he had achieved on the farm, but he couldn't help but feel as if he was letting his father down whenever Eli Yoder took the grand prize.

But this year would be different, Joseph thought with a smile.

A loss was always tragic for the community, and Joseph sympathized with the family. But since the day Eli Yoder had passed away, Joseph couldn't stop thinking about the opportunity it would bring for him. Without Eli Yoder contending for the grand prize at the fall festival, the prize was as good as delivered.

He was tired of being the second runner-up and winning wouldn't only secure him enough money to lay new irrigation pipes in his fields, but it could help him pay for much needed fertilizer for next year. *Your crop is only as good as your soil*, was something Joseph's father had always taught him.

Every five years, his father would fertilize the fields at a great expense. The fields were two years overdue, but without a winning pumpkin, Joseph simply couldn't afford to fertilize all the fields at once. Instead, he focused his soil nutrition on one specific field.

The field where he would sow the seeds for his Atlantic Giants.

The Slaber family had always grown a variety of pumpkins. It was the multiple varieties that Joseph was sowing at the moment. He would wait until early June to sow his Atlantic Giants. That way, they would be ready for the fall fair that took place in the week leading up to Halloween.

If he had the finances, he would've offered to purchase the Yoder farm now that Eli and Rowena had passed away. Joseph reasoned it would come onto the market before long since their daughter, Hannah, could never successfully run a pumpkin farm.

Not only was it hard work, but Joseph knew a girl like Hannah would much rather spend the rest of her life comfortable than working long days in the sun.

Excited about the months ahead and the prize that was just waiting to be handed to him, Joseph sowed his last seeds for the day. He walked back to the homestead and for a moment sympathized with Hannah.

When his father had passed away, the loss had been difficult enough without Joseph even facing giving up the family farm. He couldn't imagine how hard it would be for Hannah.

He quickly reprimanded himself. Hannah wasn't his friend. In their large community, she was simply someone he saw at church, from a distance. As a farmer, he needed to focus on his harvest, not on the girl whose loss made his chances for winning better.

Chapter 3
Determination
is a Virtue

Three months later

Hannah set down the tea tray on the small table on the porch. "Three sugars, half milk?"

Her best friend, Isabel Hauptfleisch, laughed. "You know me too well."

"It's hard not to. I've known you since… forever. I actually can't remember a time when I didn't know you." Hannah offered Isabel the cup and joined her on the porch swing.

When they were younger, they would spend their afternoons on that swing. They would play, swing, learn to quilt, and talk about everything that came to mind. These days, they had less time on the swing, but they still talked about everything and anything.

"Well, I didn't know you could be a pumpkin farmer," Isabel sounded impressed. "I couldn't believe all the pumpkins on the vines when I drove up to the house. Hannah, your daed would've been proud."

Hannah smiled with melancholy. "I wish he was here to see it."

"He sees it," Isabel pointed to the clouds, "from up there."

Hannah sipped on her tea and let out a quiet sigh of gratitude. Three months ago, she had been certain she was making the mistake of her life by trying to become a pumpkin farmer, but now she couldn't help but feel she had made the right choice.

For the first few weeks, she had spent every free minute in the library in town. She had learned about soil acidity, fertilizer, weeding and everything you could think of with pumpkins. By the time she had taken Samson out to till the fields, she felt as if her head was ready to explode with information.

Whereas most of the farmers sowed their pumpkins early in May, Hannah had only sown hers in the second week of June. She wanted to make sure she had all her facts lined up before she even tilled the ground. But now, as she looked at the plump orange vegetables that dotted the fields of her property, she was grateful she had taken the time to learn everything she could to combine it with everything she had learned from her father.

Her savings account was becoming slimmer by the day and Hannah couldn't help but fear that her harvest wouldn't be good enough to provide her with income for the following year. But then, wasn't that the fear her father and every farmer had every year?

Farming pumpkins was something Hannah hadn't thought she'd ever do. Of course, she'd helped her father, but she had never thought she would go at it alone. But now that she was, it made her feel closer to her father in so many ways. She began to understood decisions he made, how he spent his days and most of all she appreciated all the hard work he had done over the years.

"I found a list of all the farm stalls where my father sold his pumpkins. Next week, when I harvest my first pumpkins, I hope they will all buy from me," Hannah said almost to herself.

Isabel nodded eagerly. "Of course they will. Your farm has a reputation for the best quality and largest pumpkins in the community. Those farm stalls will knock on your door asking for more."

Hannah laughed at her friend's optimism. "I hope so."

"There is just one thing…" Isabel trailed off. "You know that Daniel and I have been courting for some time now?"

"Jah, did he propose?" Hannah asked.

Although love was the last thing on Hannah's mind, she was happy for her friend. Ever since Daniel had asked Isabel to go on their first buggy ride together a little over two months ago, the two had been almost inseparable.

"Nee. He's friends with Joseph Slaber. He told me that Joseph is already planning on a win at the fall fair," Isabel said, shaking her head. "I can't believe he's trying to profit from your father's absence at the fair this year."

"The fall fair…" Hannah trailed off. She had been so consumed with just growing pumpkins, she hadn't even considered the fall fair and the competition her father always took part in. For years, the prize for the biggest pumpkin had either come to the Yoder farm or the Slaber's. "I completely forgot about the competition. I've been so focused on making sure that I would have pumpkins to sell, I didn't even consider entering the competition."

"Well, no one could blame you, especially not with everything you've faced this year," Isabel shrugged.

"I have to enter, Isabel. That prize money could help in more ways than one. I already have Giant Atlantic's on the vine, I just have to make sure they reach the size my father used to achieve," Hannah said almost to herself.

"Hannah, it's your first year as a pumpkin farmer. Isn't aiming for the grand prize at the fair a little too optimistic?" Isabel cautioned.

"There is a difference between optimism and determination. I am determined to continue my father's legacy, and that legacy includes competing for the giant pumpkin prize," Hannah said firmly.

Isabel shrugged. "Then I wish you the best of luck… just promise me you won't be too disappointed if you don't win."

"Of course I'll be disappointed. I can imagine Joseph Slaber is watching my every move, hoping I fail. If I win the grand prize, he will have no choice but to respect me as a pumpkin farmer. I might not be my father, but his blood runs through my veins. These pumpkins are being grown with love, and the sweat and tears from my hard work. I can't let my familye down." A sigh escaped Hannah as she shook her head. "I don't want to let them down."

Isabel reached for her hand and squeezed it tightly. "You can't let them down. Look what you've already achieved."

"Are Daniel and Joseph Slaber friends?"

Isabel nodded. "Jah, it's a shame, really. But they've been friends forever."

"So your beau's best friend is my greatest competition..." Hannah trailed off. "Guess I won't be asking you to bring him along if I run short on hands to harvest then?"

"Of course I'll bring him along. He'll work extra hard to impress me."

Their laughter blended into the cool evening air. Summer was slowly drifting towards the southern hemisphere as fall crept closer. A cool reminder to Hannah that the fall fair was only two months away. When the end of October came, she needed to have a prize pumpkin on the vine.

One that wouldn't only make her father proud, but one that would establish her as a pumpkin farmer.

All she needed now was a little luck and a lot of determination.

Chapter 4
Laying Down the Gauntlet

Joseph felt triumphant as he stopped the wagon in front of the farm stall. It was officially his first delivery for the year. Fall had chased away winter, bringing with it the cooler weather and his first pumpkin harvest.

Without having to worry about Eli Yoder and his harvests, Joseph was almost relaxed as he climbed out and turned to look at the wagon loaded with pumpkins. Every year he sold to the same vendors, but every year it would be a battle for price and territory between him and Eli. Not having Eli around to compete with, Joseph felt positive that he would have his best year yet.

With pumpkins in high demand, especially with the Englisch Halloween coming at the end of October, he could name his price. Confidently, he walked into the farm stall. His eyes scanned around for the owner when a frown creased his brow. Just to the right of the entrance there was a display of pumpkins, with a large notice board announcing pumpkin season, had arrived.

Joseph walked through the farm stall and spotted the owner near the back.

"Mr. Slaghaus, gut to see you again," Joseph greeted the man with a smile.

"Ah, Joseph…. I didn't know you were coming today," Mr. Slaghaus said a little oddly.

"My first harvest is on the wagon, and as always, you're my first stop. Would you like to come and look?" Joseph asked, gesturing towards the door.

Mr. Slaghaus shook his head with a frown. "If I knew you were coming… Joseph, I already brought this week's stock from Eli Yoder's dochder. She was just here." Mr. Slaghaus smiled. "She brought in quite the harvest, seeing as it's her first. It's her pumpkins on the display right over there."

Joseph turned slowly back to look at the pumpkin display and felt as if the earth had moved beneath him. He hadn't even for one second stopped to consider that Hannah might attempt to continue farming pumpkins, but in front of him he not only had evidence that she did but also evidence that she had her father's talent for it.

All the pumpkins were evenly sized, their color, exquisite, with no sign of parasites. He pasted a smile to his face as he turned back to Mr. Slaghaus. "I see, then I'll stop by again next week."

Mr. Slaghaus chuckled. "You do that Joseph, and remember, the early bird gets the worm."

Joseph grunted with irritation as he walked out of the farm stall. He wasn't supposed to have competition this year, and he wasn't supposed to be outdone by a girl. Especially not a girl that has never sowed or harvested pumpkins before.

Something he'd been doing since he could remember.

Angry, frustrated and more than a little disappointed, he walked towards his wagon when he noticed another wagon coming out from behind the farm stall. Holding the reins was none other than Hannah Yoder.

Without hesitation, Joseph walked up and stood right in front of the buggy, causing her to pull on the reins. "What do you think you're doing?"

For a moment, Joseph couldn't help but be surprised by how beautiful she had become. In his mind, Hannah was still the little girl that had been three years behind him in school. But holding the reins and looking at him with narrowed eyes, sat a beautiful woman. Her hair was the color of melted chocolate, her eyes the color of the sky. But it wasn't only her eyes that appealed to Joseph on a personal level, it was the combination of a pert stubborn nose, a generous mouth, and a sleek jawline.

"I'm driving my wagon; would you mind moving?" She snapped at him from on high.

Joseph crossed his arms and planted his feet. "Not before you and I have a word. I'm sorry to hear about your parents, but if you intend on farming pumpkins, you need to understand something. Mr. Slaghaus is my vendor, not yours."

"Really?" Hannah asked, tilting her head curiously. "Because he was more than happy to buy from me since you hadn't bothered to deliver him your harvest yet."

"I was an hour later than you…" Joseph huffed. "How did you…" Joseph trailed off, not knowing which question to ask first.

How did she learn to grow pumpkins?

How did she find out where to sell them?

And why was she looking so pretty when she was delivering pumpkins?

"You wanted to ask something?" Hannah asked, cocking her brow, looking bored by his interruption.

"Jah, where are you headed next?" Joseph asked off the top of his head.

Hannah chuckled. "To the next name on my father's list of vendors. You don't really think I'm going to tell you, do you?"

"It just so happens that your daed and I used the same vendors. First come, first served. You might have harvested your pumpkins, but I'll make sure you don't sell another one. See that horse? He's just as stubborn as I am and as fast as a fox and strong as an ox. We'll beat you to every vendor, every time." He couldn't help but smile sarcastically, although he knew it was probably wrong.

"Really?" Hannah asked, as if his display of dominance thoroughly entertained her. "Do you see this horse here? She's as quick as an eagle in flight and doesn't tire easily. We'll just have to see who wins?"

"Fine, but one rule," Joseph laid down the gauntlet. "If you arrive and I'm already selling, you leave."

"Same counts if you arrive after me," Hannah said with a narrowed look. "Now, if you don't mind, get out of the way!"

Joseph held her gaze for a few more seconds, as if just to make sure that she knew he wasn't intending to back down before he stepped out of the way. He watched her drive off with her wagon, feeling robbed of his profit at the sight of her half empty buggy.

Except for being his most reliable vendor, Mr. Slaghaus also always bought the most pumpkins. If he wanted to sell his entire wagon load, he would need to make sure he hit the biggest vendors before Hannah.

It felt like déjà vu from years before, except this time he wasn't competing with Eli Yoder. This time he was competing with a beautiful woman that hadn't only caught him off guard, but had made his heart skip a beat with excitement at the thought of competing with her.

It made little sense, but then the fact that Hannah Yoder had brought in her own harvest made little sense either.

Chapter 5
A Half-Triumph

Hannah arrived home late that afternoon.

Her hands were blistered from holding the reins for most of the day, her back aching from moving pumpkins and her skin wind-burnt from the cold. If they had emptied her wagon it would've all been worth it, but her wagon was still half-full.

She knew it was a triumph that she had sown and harvested her own pumpkins and sold more than half of her first harvest, but that also meant only half the income she would need for the next year.

It was a bitter-sweet ending to a hard day on the road.

Once she had brushed down the horse and fed and watered it, she headed inside to put on a pot of coffee. She wanted to warm her hands, her body, and put some ointment on her face. Tomorrow she would remember sunblock and moisturizer, she promised herself as she glanced at the buggy again.

She refused to unload the pumpkins and reload them again, which meant she had no choice but to go selling again tomorrow, even if it meant stopping her wagon on the side of the road and selling to passersby.

Just as soon as the pot of coffee finished brewing, there was a knock on the door. The last thing Hannah felt like was having visitors, but when she opened the door and saw Isabel standing on the porch, she nearly burst out in tears with gratitude.

"Hannah! What happened to you?" Isabel's voice held a high-pitch tone of concern.

"Windburn. I didn't expect to spend all day in the wagon. I'll take better care tomorrow." Hannah opened the door to let her friend in.

"I thought I'd stop by and find out how it went… but I see there are still pumpkins on the wagon?" Isabel, comfortable in her friend's home, poured herself a cup of coffee and joined Hannah at the kitchen table.

"Jah," Hannah sighed heavily. "When I found my daed's list of vendors, I didn't realize it was the same vendors that Joseph Slaber frequents…"

"Ach nee… What happened?" Isabel frowned curiously.

"I stopped at the first vendor and sold one fifth of my harvest. Just as I left, feeling triumphant and confident that I could actually do this, I was stopped by Slaber." Hannah groaned. "After a show-down no less, he made it clear that I would never succeed and that he would reach the vendors quicker than I could find their names on my daed's list."

"Nee!" Isabel seemed intrigued.

"Jah. Needless to say, I did sell to a few vendors, but Joseph had already been to most of them. Which means he probably sold all his pumpkins, and I came home with about half of my harvest." Hannah shook her head. "Isabel, if I don't sell my pumpkins, what's the use in growing them?

Joseph has had a relationship with these vendors for years. I don't."

Isabel reached for Hannah's hand. "You're right, you don't. But your father did. Don't try to reinvent the wheel, Hannah, just keep it turning."

"How am I supposed to keep the wheel turning if my wheels turn slower than his?" Hannah's voice was laced with frustration.

"Perhaps you could leave earlier, or maybe... maybe you should talk to Joseph and suggest you divide the vendors between the two of you. That way you both have equal opportunity to sell your pumpkins?" Isabel suggested with a hopeful smile.

Hannah scoffed. "You mean ask him to share? He's about as willing to share his vendors with me as he is for me to grow pumpkins. He expected I would rather sell the farm than grow pumpkins, and now he's out to make sure that I fail. I will not beg him for mercy."

"That's my best friend talking," Isabel laughed. "If you're not going beg him for mercy, then you'll have to up your game."

"How?" Hannah asked with a shake of her head. "I can't do much more than I did today."

"Pray on it. I'm sure Gott will have the answers you need. He'll give you strength to carry on your daed's legacy, Hannah, you just have to ask."

Hannah nodded. "I hope so."

"In the meantime, how are your Atlantic Giants looking? Do you think you have a winner on the vine?" Isabel asked eagerly.

Hannah shrugged. "They all look the same to me. There's a month to grow them yet. They're going into their peak growth phase now, so time will tell. I've removed the fruit from the secondary vines on each one, so each vine only has one fruit to focus all its nutrients and minerals on."

"Sounds like you know what you're talking about," Isabel said, impressed.

Hannah sighed with a sad smile. "All these years, I helped Mamm around the house, never once paying attention to how Daed farmed the pumpkins. Now I wish I could've learned from him. All I have are a few notes on where to buy seeds and which varieties, but it's as if he kept all his experience and knowledge locked up in his mind. I'm working with what I learned from books, and I hope that's going to be enough."

"I'm sure it will be. Even if you don't win the grand prize at the fall fair, just that you're competing is impressive," Isabel assured her.

Hannah smiled at her friend, knowing she was right, but deep-down Hannah couldn't help but hope for a win. At least then Joseph would stop treating her like an errant child that's playing on the wrong playground.

Chapter 6
All is Fair in Love
& War

Joseph was working in the field the next day when he saw Daniel pull up in front of the barn. He dusted his hands on the seat of his pants and headed in that direction.

Joseph and Daniel had been friends since childhood, and no one understood better than Daniel how important the farm and growing pumpkins were to Joseph. After yesterday's disappointing sales, he could use Daniel's advice.

"Hullo!" Joseph called out as Daniel climbed out of his buggy. "Aren't you working today?"

"Hullo! Jah, but I had some errands in town and thought I'd stop by," Daniel nodded, tipping his hat in greeting.

"Gut of you," Joseph nodded with a smile. "Would you like some kaffe?"

"Jah, why not?" Daniel agreed before he stopped and caught sight of the wagon in the barn. "Isn't that last week's harvest?"

Joseph rolled his eyes. "Jah, it is. I'll tell you about that in a moment."

Once they both had a cup of coffee, they meandered back to the barn where the wagon stood half-full of pumpkins. "Eli Yoder's dochder took it upon herself to farm pumpkins."

Daniel laughed. "Did you expect anything less? You surely didn't think she'd sell the familye farm after losing both her parents?"

"Why not? A woman's place is in the house, not in the field," Joseph scoffed.

"A hundred years ago perhaps, but these days it's all about equality. Now tell me, how did Eli Yoder's dochder, whose place is in the house, cause you to come home with half your harvest?" Daniel asked in a mocking tone.

"She arrived at my biggest vendors before I could. I warned her I was going to outrun her with my wagon, but she beat me to it." Joseph hated that he sounded like a child who got robbed of his favorite toy.

Daniel's laughter made him feel even worse. "Ach Joseph, surely it's not that bad. You competed with Eli every year, so how is it any different to competing with his dochder?"

"Because I wasn't expecting competition this year. I was expecting to sell all my harvest, to win the grand prize at the fair, and all without having to even consider that I might have competition," Joseph admitted.

"What are you going to do?" Daniel asked, taking a sip of his coffee.

"I'm going to beat her, of course. I just have to figure out how." Joseph thought for a moment before a smile curved the corners of his mouth. "Isn't the saying "all is fair in love and war"? Then I'm declaring war on Hannah Yoder."

Daniel frowned. "That saying applies to the Englisch. We don't believe in war, remember?"

"Perhaps not when lives are involved, but we're talking about pumpkins," Joseph said firmly.

"And her livelihood," Daniel reminded him. "She just lost her parents, Joseph. Perhaps you should go easy on her this year. It's her first year growing pumpkins, and she's still grieving; I don't think she needs you to make things even harder on her."

"It's fair play, Daniel. If she wants to become a pumpkin farmer, it would be wrong of me to make it easy on her this year and then next year make her face the reality. Rather, she learns now before she becomes too invested," Joseph shrugged as if his reasoning made sense. "Besides, it's not sabotage, it's just... a little creative marketing if she finds her wagon with a broken wheel."

"Joseph Slaber, you won't!" Daniel cried out, horrified.

"Nee," Joseph sighed, "I won't. But I will harvest a day earlier this week and hopefully beat her to the vendors. I need to do something, Daniel, or I won't have an income to make ends meet."

Daniel shrugged before he let out a chuckle. "So the competition is on. May the best pumpkin farmer win."

"May the best man win indeed," Joseph said, holding up his mug.

"What are you going to do with the pumpkins in the barn?" Daniel asked, nodding towards the wagon that was half-full.

"I have to go into town tomorrow to do some errands, then I'll drop them off at the soup kitchen. At least they won't go to waste."

"Gut mann," Daniel approved of his plan. "I have to get going. Just remember, Joseph, do nothing you'll regret later. The Lord blesses and protects those that care for their neighbor, but he punishes the selfish."

"Jah, jah," Joseph nodded. "Go on, I have some Atlantic Giants to take care of."

"How are they looking?" Daniel inquired about the prize vines.

"Gut enough to win me the grand prize," Joseph said confidently. "She might beat me at selling to the vendors, but with the grand prize at the fall fair, that prize is as gut as mine. Not everyone can grow an Atlantic Giant to reach its full potential, but I can."

"Careful, you've underestimated her once. Don't do it again," Daniel warned as he climbed into his buggy and took the reins. "Gut luck my friend. Sounds like you might just need it."

Joseph waved goodbye to his friend but didn't feel concerned in the least. Now that he knew what he was up against, he could plan his victory.

Besides, he couldn't imagine that Hannah knew anything about growing prize pumpkins.

Chapter 7
Humiliation Beckons Failure

Hannah couldn't remember her father as desperate to sell pumpkins as she was today.

After doing her morning chores, she had taken the reins of the wagon with blistered hands. The wind was biting, slicing through her coat as she stopped on the side of the road. For a moment she considered going home and waiting for better weather, but tomorrow there would be more work that needed to be done.

If she wanted to sell the pumpkins, she couldn't sell the day before, she had no choice but to sell them today. Hannah put up the sign her father had always used at the fair and discounted the price, hoping it would help her sell the pumpkins faster.

With her sign in place, she climbed back into the wagon and draped a blanket over her knees. It helped a little to ward off the cold, but she couldn't help but wish that she had brought a flask of cocoa or coffee along.

It was a full hour before the first car pulled over. The Englisch couple were clearly tourists driving through. They had more questions about her culture and her lifestyle than they did about her pumpkins.

When they finally bought one pumpkin, Hannah couldn't help but feel they had only bought the pumpkin out of kindness.

The second car revealed an Englisch mother with her two young children. She bought two pumpkins and offered to give Hannah her pumpkin pie recipe. When Hannah assured her it wasn't necessary, the lady continued to explain to Hannah about spices. As if the Amish had never used a single space in their three hundred years of existence.

Finally, she saw a buggy approach in the distance and felt a little relieved that it wasn't more Englischers. She had nothing against Englischers, but she hated feeling as if they pitied her for standing on the side of the road exposed to the elements.

She waved when the driver waved to her in advance. Only when the buggy stopped beside hers did she recognize the driver.

Joseph Slaber.

A wave of anxiety rushed over her. She didn't want to argue with him again, not after the way he had made it clear yesterday that she was an imposter in the pumpkin business.

"Guten mayrie, Hannah," Joseph said with a smile that reminded her of a wolf. "Opening a roadside pumpkin stand, I see?"

Hannah seethed inwardly. "Guten mayrie Joseph. Selling pumpkins, that's what I'm doing. Or are you going to claim this road as *yours* as well?"

Joseph chuckled. "I'm sorry to see you're in such bad spirits. Just remember, pumpkin season has just begun. I hope you will not be in a bad mood for all of it."

"I'm not...." Hannah huffed out an angry sigh. "If you're not planning on buying a pumpkin, just go."

"Very well then, best of luck, Hannah. Remember to steer clear of my vendors!" Joseph called back as he waved to her.

Hannah let out a silent groan.

How did her father put up with Joseph Slaber all these years?

By the time noon rolled around, Hannah was thoroughly negative. She couldn't spend all of her time sitting on the side of the road because Joseph Slaber claimed the vendors for himself. She didn't know what she was going to do, but she needed a plan.

Since a car pulled over only every hour or so, Hannah used most of that time to pray. She cried now and then, wondering if she was strong enough to meet the challenge that Gott had laid at her door.

By the time evening rolled around, she had five pumpkins left in her wagon.

A black Englisch car rolled up, and an Englischer climbed out wearing a suit. Fear raced down Hannah's spine. She had seen no signs forbidding her from selling pumpkins from a wagon, but you never knew.

The last thing she needed now was to be given a fine, a fine she couldn't afford to pay.

The man approached her with a warm smile. "Hello miss. How are you today?"

"Hullo, I'm gut denke," Hannah replied cautiously.

"I'm very gut. I just came from a Conference of Faith, so I feel renewed in both spirit and soul. You must be cold if you've been sitting here all day?"

Hannah nodded. "A little."

"Well then, let me help you out of your misery. How many pumpkins do you have left and what do they price at?"

Hannah told him she had five left and named her price. To her surprise, the man pulled out his wallet and handed her more than the price of five pumpkins. "I'll take them all. My congregation's soup kitchen could always use more vegetables."

Hannah wasn't sure if she should cry or smile with gratitude. "Denke."

She was about to climb out of the wagon when the man held up his hand. "I'll take care of it. Don't bother climbing down."

Hannah watched as he carried the five pumpkins to the trunk of his car, wondering if he was an angel that had just been sent by Gott to give her hope.

When he said goodbye, Hannah knew he was just that.

"You take care now miss and remember Jeremiah 29:11 *God knows the plans he has for you, plans to prosper you and not to harm you.*"

Hannah repeated the verse in her mind all the way home. Regardless of Joseph's condescending words and the competition they posed for each other, Gott had plans for her.

Chapter 8
A New Plan

After selling the other half of her wagon load of pumpkins by the side of the road the week before, Hannah knew she needed a better plan this week. Driving all day and spending another day standing by the side of the road kept her away from the farm too much.

She had prayed for the last few days every single night for a solution to her problem. If she was going to spend most of her time battling for vendors with Joseph, she wouldn't have enough time to get her work done around the farm.

Hannah spent most of Saturday harvesting the new pumpkins that were ready. She wanted to leave first thing Monday morning to beat Joseph to the biggest vendors. These first few harvests were small compared to the harvesting she would do before the fall festival. But their income was just as vital.

On Saturday afternoon she had gone into town to do some marketing and right there in the produce aisle of the supermarket God answered her prayers. Her plan to chase after vendors and try to beat Joseph completely evaporated as a new plan emerged.

Hannah had prayed for guidance in church on Sunday and had returned home to spend the day checking numbers. The more she made the calculations, the more she realized her plan would work.

That was why on a brisk Monday morning she wasn't headed to Mr. Slaghaus. Instead, Hannah and her wagon, loaded with pumpkins, were heading into town. If she could get the supermarket to buy her small weekly harvests every week at a lower price than the farm stalls, it would secure her income and save her time.

She might earn less per pound for her produce, but at least she would have the security of knowing they would sell her harvests. And if she sold everything to the local grocer, it would amount to the same amount as spending days on the road, trying to sell to vendors that played her and Joseph's price per pound off against each other.

When she stopped in front of the grocer, she couldn't help but feel a little nervous. She had spent her life cleaning and cooking and doing laundry—talking business wasn't something she was familiar with. But if she wanted to keep her family farm, she would simply need to familiarize herself with it today.

A short while later, she sat across from the store owner in his office.

"You want me to buy my pumpkins directly from you instead of from the produce distributors?" he asked with a curious look.

"Jah, might I ask what you pay per pound at the moment?" Hannah asked, trying not to reveal how nervous she was or how desperate she was for him to say yes.

He mentioned a price per pound that made Hannah breathe a little easier. She had estimated it around that number.

"I will sell my pumpkins for 10% below what you're paying. I can deliver a wagon load to you every Monday. Not only is it better for you because your clients are buying freshly harvested pumpkins grown organically, but you're also supporting a local farmer."

The store owner frowned and shook his head with curiosity. "No one from your community has ever approached me. If they had, I might have supported the farming community a long time ago."

"Now that I have, does that mean we have a deal?" Hannah asked as she stood up and held out her hand.

The store owner chuckled. "Miss Yoder, we certainly do. There is just one thing: if I don't sell the number of pumpkins you're delivering, who is going to take the loss?"

Hannah shrugged. "You will sell them. Pumpkin season has just begun, and everyone is eager to make pumpkin pies and stock up for Halloween. Seventy percent of the pumpkins I grow are jack-o'-lanterns—carve a few and inspire your customers to buy more. Besides, if your pumpkins are the best-priced in town, you'll have no problem selling them."

The store owner chuckled with a smile as he shook Hannah's hand. "You're right, Miss Yoder. I look forward to doing business with you. You can pull your wagon around back and I'll have my men take care of unloading. Once they've all been weighed, I'll pay you for the batch."

"Denke," Hannah said, feeling relieved. She had worked out worst-case-scenario prices for her calculations, but the store owner was offering her more than she had planned on. Which meant not only didn't she have to spend two days away from the farm, but she would sell all her pumpkins and she wasn't required to carry a single one.

"You're welcome to have a cup of coffee at our coffee shop while you wait—on the house, of course."

Hannah's smile broadened. "Denke, I'd like that very much."

An hour later, Hannah was driving home with an empty wagon. For the first time since she had sown her first seeds, she felt as if she was doing something right. Not only did she have fields and fields with pumpkins on the vine, but now she had secured an outlet without having to compete with Joseph.

Victory was even sweeter than she could've imagined.

She was nearly home when she noticed Joseph driving towards her. She hid her smile, not wanting him to think she liked him in any way. He was adorable trying to claim all the vendors for himself.

"Hullo fellow farmer! Let's see who goes home with an empty wagon today!" Joseph called out sarcastically.

As he neared, Hannah simply smiled at him with delight. "Jah, let's do!" She pointed to her empty wagon and laughed all the way home.

Chapter 9
A Bump in the Road

Joseph unloaded the pallets and smiled at how large his vines were. The recent rains that had surprised them the week before had truly been a blessing for his pumpkins. It saved him the trouble of watering the vines, and could see the growth spurt in the leaves.

He set out the pallets, one at each Atlantic Giant vine.

The key to growing prize pumpkins, he'd learned long ago, was to only grow one pumpkin on each vine. Early in the growing process, he would remove most of the flowers. Each flower became a fruit, so it was essential that he forced the vine to put all its energy into producing one giant fruit instead of many smaller ones.

Now that he had all twenty of his prize vines bearing one fruit each, it was time to lift them off the ground. Nothing was more disappointing than growing a prize-winning fruit, only to lift it during harvest and to find the bottom half rotten.

It was essential that he lifted his prize giants off the ground while he could still lift them on his own. That was what he used the pallets for. He began lifting his first pumpkin by clearing the ground of weeds before he laid down the pallet. Once the pallet was in place, he would lay an inch thick bed of sand beneath it, to keep the moisture in the ground and not on the pallet.

Once that was done, he placed a large piece of mill fabric that would allow the water to drain through if it rained, before placing the pumpkin on top of it.

Only when he stood back and looked at the size of the pumpkin compared to the pallet did Joseph feel cold sweat bead on his forehead.

His pumpkins should've been much larger by now.

He pulled out his measuring tape and measured the pumpkin, feeling even more disappointed when his suspicions were confirmed. In the years before, his pumpkins were at least 10% bigger when they lifted them than they were now.

Joseph scratched his head, wondering where he had gone wrong this year. The answer came to him at once.

Fertilizer.

He had been fertilizing patches of soil here and there as they needed it, but without the prize money, he simply couldn't afford to fertilize all his fields. Joseph drove the wagon back to the barn and collected some fertilizer and straw. To give his pumpkins the best chance of becoming prize winners, he needed to tend to the weeding at the base of the vine immediately. After he had done that, he would fertilize it properly before laying down a bed of straw.

There was only one problem, he realized as he looked for his fertilizer and only came up with an empty bag. He didn't have any. For a moment, Joseph debated between finishing the task he had begun by lifting his pumpkins off the ground, or to drive into town for fertilizer. Both were just as important.

After debating for a few moments, he went to buy the fertilizer instead. Without fertilizer, there would be no prize pumpkins for his pallets to hold.

Joseph quickly diverted his attention from the vines to the problem at hand. While he hitched up the buggy, he tried to consider any other factors that might affect the growth of his pumpkins. He was doing everything he had done the year before. In fact, last year he didn't even have the blessing of rain.

A sigh escaped him as he took the reins of the horse and called to him. "Step up."

The horse walked before it flawlessly moved over into an easy trot as they headed towards town.

Joseph wasn't sure what the reason was for his smaller pumpkins, but he knew that if he wanted to win the prize money at the fair he'd need to focus harder on the Atlantic Giants and less on the jack-o'-lanterns he sold every week.

A frown creased his brow as he thought about the latter. Hannah came to mind with her empty wagon from a few days before. It had surprised him that her wagon was empty so early in the morning. He had been even more surprised that she hadn't sold to any of their usual vendors. Everywhere he stopped, they were eagerly awaiting his delivery.

A small smile curved his mouth as he came to a conclusion. The reason her wagon had been empty was because she hadn't had many pumpkins to sell. Perhaps that first week had been beginner's luck and now that the real competition had begun, she had barely any pumpkins left on the vine.

He could only hope that it meant that she didn't have any prize winners either.

With the money he had made from selling last week's harvest, he could buy the fertilizer he needed and when his plants had the right nutients, his Atlantic Giants would grow into prize winners.

Chapter 10
Privileged Information

Hannah's Atlantic Giants had been lifted onto beds of well-draining sand, the way her father had always done it in the past. Although she had read about farmers using pallets and beds of mill fabric, this was one thing she remembered about her father's way of growing giant pumpkins.

The field where she grew her giants looked as if there were large white mounds protruding from the ground with cherries on top. Only the cherries were bright orange pumpkins that she hoped would result in her prize win at the fair.

She had pruned back her vines to make sure energy was directed towards the fruit and she had even spun the white tarps over her prize winners, to make sure the sun didn't impact their color or their growth.

All she needed to do now was take as good care of the vines as she could. After spending most of the morning in the library to research which fertilizers her vines needed at this stage of the growth process, she headed to the co-op to buy bone meal and potassium-rich fertilizer.

Now that she had a confirmed vendor who would buy her smaller weekly harvests, Hannah felt confident about the rest of the pumpkin season. She had enough jack-o'-lanterns on the vine to keep supplying the grocer every week, and she would still have plenty to sell at the fair.

Hannah now had more time for caring for the vines and even installed her own drip water irrigation system that delivered water directly to the base of her Atlantic Giants, instead of having to water them by hand.

She might not have been a pumpkin farmer when she inherited her parents' farm, but she was quickly learning and couldn't help but feel proud of herself for everything she had accomplished in such a short time.

As she walked through the co-op, she priced the irrigation pipes. If she won the grand prize at the fall fair, she might even splurge and install her own irrigation drip system the following year. The system was very simple. Simple enough that Hannah had done it herself without spending too much money.

She had simply attached a hose to the water tank that now led to her prized vines. From there, she attached the hose to an irrigation pipe that lay vertical and allowed three other irrigation pipes to attach horizontally. Holes were made on the irrigation pipe only at the base of her prized vines. Which meant no water would touch the leaves and the soil would be watered where it was needed most, directly above the roots.

Her father used to dig shallow water troughs around his prized vines and allow them to fill with water before draining naturally into the soil. But Hannah couldn't help but feel her method was more effective and less laborious.

She had just retrieved the bonemeal she needed and was heading towards the fertilizer aisle when she recognized

Jacob Slaber's voice. Hannah stopped right in her tracks, curious what Jacob bought from the co-op. He was in the next aisle, talking to another Amish man whose voice Hannah didn't recognize.

"Now that Eli Yoder isn't here to give you a hard time, you're going to win the grand prize at the fair this year?" the man asked.

"I hope so. Actually, I was hoping to ask you a little advice pertaining to the grand prize," Jacob's voice lowered slightly.

"Of course, I've been giving advice on fertilizers my entire life," the Amish man replied.

Hannah nodded to herself, realizing Joseph was talking to Brahm Holshausen. Brahm had been working at the co-op forever.

"My Atlantic Giants... I've done everything the same as I do every year, but they seem to be a little... smaller than they usually are this time of year," Joseph admitted.

Hannah's heart skipped a beat. This conversation could help her win the grand prize. She held her breath and listened to every word that Brahm offered as advice.

"You pruned the flowers, I take it? You water them frequently? How about fertilizer? Did you fertilize your ground sufficiently?"

"I'm not sure. I did fertilize, but only at the base of the root. I've taken some potassium fertilizer and bonemeal, which I'm going to work in at the base of the vine."

"Are you watering it frequently enough?" Brahm asked.

"Jah, every day," Joseph answered.

"And you have straw around the base of the vine?"

"Jah. Hopefully the potassium gives it the growth spurt it needs," Joseph admitted hopefully.

"I'm sure it will, Joseph. You've always known your way around prize vines, you just have to keep doing what you're doing."

Hannah stood in the next aisle and knew from the conversation that fertilizer wasn't Joseph's problem. After learning everything she could about growing pumpkins and nurturing giant pumpkins, she couldn't help but feel a little triumphant that she knew something he didn't.

A smile curved her lips, knowing that he was having trouble with the size of his pumpkins now, and fertilizer wouldn't fix the problem. Instead, he won't even have a prize pumpkin to enter at the fair.

For a moment she felt as if victory was in her reach, but something nagged at the back of her mind. Enough so that it wouldn't be a fair win if she didn't speak up.

Hannah at first refused to abide to the voice in her mind. If the tables were reversed, Joseph wouldn't have offered advice to help her beat him. Instead, he would've probably given her the wrong advice.

She walked away, planning on returning to the fertilizer aisle when Joseph was gone, when she stopped mid step.

All is fair in love and war, but if she didn't speak up, this wouldn't be a fair war.

Chapter 11
Unexpected Advice

Joseph was certain fertilizer was his problem. Now that Brahm confirmed it, he had no choice but to buy more than he had intended to. If he didn't, all his prize vines would disappoint him this year.

"I'll take two bags of bone meal Brahm, and two potassium fertilizers," Joseph said to Brahm as another person came walking down the aisle.

"Hullo Joseph, hullo Brahm," Hannah greeted them both with a warm smile.

For a moment, Joseph was taken aback. Why was she being friendly? Had he been wrong? Did she sell more pumpkins than he did and now she was here to rub it in his face? Even if she was, she still looked beautiful as she stopped in front of them.

"Hannah," Brahm said, a little flustered. "Didn't expect to see you here. I hear you've followed in your daed's footsteps?"

"Jah, it's been a challenge, but I'm enjoying it." Hannah smiled warmly at Brahm and, for a moment, Joseph wished she had smiled at him in that way.

When she turned and looked directly at him, Joseph squared his shoulders, ready for the attack she was no doubt about to unleash on him. "Your problem isn't fertilizer."

"What?" Joseph asked, surprised.

"I couldn't help but overhear your conversation just now. You think your pumpkins aren't growing right because they need more fertilizer. That's not your problem," Hannah repeated.

"It's rude to eavesdrop," Joseph snapped.

Sensing there was an argument about to unfold, Brahm made an excuse and disappeared into the depths of the co-op.

"It's not eavesdropping when you're talking and I am in the next aisle. I didn't know you were here; I didn't intend to overhear your conversation," Hannah said simply. She glanced at the fertilizers and shrugged. "Adding potassium at this stage of the growth cycle can't hurt, neither can bone meal, but that still isn't your problem."

"How would you know?" Joseph snapped irritably. "You've been growing pumpkins for what, three months now? I've been growing them my whole life. I think in identifying problems, I'm a little more qualified to dole out advice than you."

Hannah shook her head and held his gaze. "Just because we're both pumpkin farmers and we're both competing for the grand prize at the fair, doesn't mean we can't help each other. If you don't want my help, then fine. But don't pout when I win the prize at the fair."

Hannah turned on her heel and walked away. Joseph wasn't sure what was it about her that infuriated him more.

That she was pretty and kind, or that he wanted her to fail and knew it was wrong.

Either way, his curiosity got the better of him. "Fine! What is my problem, then?" he called out after her.

Hannah stopped and turned. She looked at him with an arched brow. "If that is how you ask for advice, I'd rather not waste my breath. But just this once, I'll look past your lack of manners."

She walked back to him and stopped just a few feet from him. Joseph couldn't help but feel taken aback. Although his father hadn't been around for years, it felt as if his father had just scolded him for being rude.

"I'm sorry. I meant… I'd like to hear what you think my problem is?" Joseph asked, this time without acid lacing his voice.

Hannah smiled. "You said you're watering your pumpkins every day?"

"Jah, they're thirsty fruits. I'm sure you know that watering is the most important part of growing Atlantic Giants?"

Hannah nodded. "Jah, and I also know that if the water drenches your leaves and your fruit, it will rot. The same goes for your root system."

"What?" Joseph asked, not following her trail of thought.

"We've had a lot of rain over the last few weeks. I take it you water your crops every day because that's how you've always done it. You see rain as an extra bonus when you have fruit on the vine?" Hannah asked without even a hint of sarcasm in her voice.

"Jah," Joseph nodded, wondering how she understood his reasoning when she barely knew him at all.

"That's your problem. Pumpkins need a lot of water, especially to establish a good root system, but too much water can be deadly. With all the rain we've had, I've only had to water my Atlantic Giants every third day."

"Every third day?" Joseph asked, surprised. "That doesn't sound right…"

Hannah nodded. "But it is. If you test your soil for moisture before watering, you'll realize that too. If your soil is too wet, it robs the soil of oxygen and dilutes your nutrients. So it wouldn't matter how much you fertilize it, the roots won't absorb it if the soil is too wet."

Joseph couldn't believe that Hannah was even giving him advice, let alone teaching him something about pumpkins he didn't know. "So the rain is at fault?"

"A little, along with your over-watering. It would be best to wait on the fertilizer for a few days. Let the soil dry out a little first. Test it by putting your finger in the ground. If you can still feel the soil is moist, one inch deep, that means you need to hold off on watering," Hannah explained.

Joseph shook his head. "Why are you telling me this?"

Hannah smiled at him warmly. "Because just because we're competing doesn't mean it doesn't have to be fair." A soft laugh escaped her. "If I win the grand prize at the fair, I want to know it's because I won it fair and square, not because I knew you had a problem and didn't offer to help."

Joseph smiled at her. For a moment he was completely lost in her gaze. For a few brief seconds, there weren't pumpkins, a grand prize, or even vendors between them.

There was nothing except a feeling of being drawn to each other.

Joseph had never experienced something like that before. "You're not like I expected you to be."

Her cheeks flushed slightly before she laughed. "I'm not sure what you expected, but I'll take that as a compliment. Good luck with Atlantic Giants, Joseph."

She grabbed a bag of potassium fertilizer and walked away, leaving Joseph both confused and intrigued by his newest competition.

Chapter 12
Opportunity or Threat

When Hannah arrived home later that afternoon, she was eager to get her fingers in the dirt.

She felt good for giving Joseph advice and even better that she actually knew what she was talking about. She understood that most of the farmers in the area had learned from their fathers and their fathers had learned from their fathers before them.

But Hannah didn't have that privilege.

Her father had always spoken about how Hannah's husband would one day take over the farm. Her father had talked as if he had years ahead of him still. Little did he and Hannah know that his time with her would be cut short.

She might not have had the privilege to learn from her father, but she felt good knowing that her research and hours and hours spent in the library had amounted to something.

Advice she would've never known to give before.

When she had spoken to Joseph, she had seen the surprise in his eyes. He had been skeptical, thinking she wanted to sabotage him. But once she had explained and the competitiveness flew out the window, Joseph seemed to be a different man entirely.

Hannah felt a smile curve her mouth as she shifted the bag of bonemeal onto her shoulder.

Joseph was an attractive man, a very attractive man.

She hadn't noticed it before because she had been too busy trying to prove herself, but when he smiled at her in the co-op with gratitude in his gaze, something inside Hannah had cracked open. She wasn't sure if it was an unexplored emotion or the barriers she had put up since losing her parents. All she knew was that she felt different when he had looked at her in that way.

Hannah set down the bag of bonemeal beside her prized vines and remembered something Isabel had told her when she and Daniel had begun to court.

'I don't know how to explain it. All I know is that it felt as if I've spent every moment of my life surviving until that minute. When he looked at me, I felt truly alive.'

The memory and the words caught Hannah off guard. Romance and Joseph didn't belong in the same train of thought, they didn't even belong in the same universe. Regardless of the way he had made her feel in the co-op, she needed to remind herself that he was her biggest competition.

If she didn't focus on her farm and her pumpkins, Joseph would be the reason for her demise. He would profit not only from her parents' tragic accident, but he would profit from her failure as well. She couldn't allow herself to think of him as anything but the villain in her story.

Joseph Slaber might have accepted her advice, but that didn't mean he was going to back down if he had a bigger pumpkin than Hannah when the fall fair came around.

Hannah pushed all thoughts of Joseph, including his handsome smile, warm brown eyes, and broad shoulders, aside and sliced open the bag of bonemeal. Using her fingers, instead of a gardening tool, she carefully worked the bonemeal into the base of every vine.

If she used gardening tools, she risked cutting the roots and hurting them. If she used her fingers, she would immediately feel if she was near the roots. Bonemeal was good for the vines, but direct contact, or too much contact, might cause a dead vine.

Just like her interactions with Joseph. A little interaction was good, it kept them on good footing. But too much interaction… and she just might watch him walk away with the grand prize at the fall fair.

A heavy sigh escaped her as she realized her thoughts had trailed to Joseph again.

Hannah stood up from the ground and brushed the dirt off her knees. She glanced over the fields of pumpkins that still needed to be harvested and made a vow to herself right there and then.

She would not let Joseph slip past her barriers again.

She didn't care if she had felt *alive* when he had looked at her in that certain way. She didn't have time to even consider that now.

It was pumpkin growing time, and nothing else mattered.

As she walked back to the house, she remembered a fond memory of her mother. Her mother had coaxed her many times to attend Sunday singings, but Hannah had always refused. For Hannah, Sunday Singings were where you went when you had a sweetheart in mind. She didn't want to wait outside a barn only to walk herself home in the dark.

But her mother had a different opinion.

Her mother had believed that you had to open yourself to the opportunity to receive it. What would her mother have said of Joseph?

An opportunity or a threat?

Chapter 13
Returning the Favor

The fall fair was only a couple of weeks away.

Joseph knew that if he won the grand prize, he could sell his pumpkins there for a better price per pound. That's why when he harvested jack-o'-lanterns over the weekend, he only harvested the biggest of the crop.

He would leave the rest on the vine, giving them a chance to mature even more before the fall fair. There was that, and there was the fear that Hannah would beat him to his best vendors again today and he would return home with a wagonload of pumpkins like he did a couple of weeks ago.

Ever since he had bumped into her at the co-op a few days ago, Joseph was having a hard time keeping Hannah off his mind. He couldn't understand why she would offer him advice, when so much was on the line for her this year.

Not only did she need to prove herself as pumpkin farmer to the farm stall owners and members of the community, but he knew through the community gossip that she needed the grand prize money.

Cautious of her advice, fearing that she might try to sabotage him, he'd stopped by the library on his way home to do some research. Indeed, Hannah's advice had been true. He had been over-watering his Atlantic Giants.

After two days of withholding water, he could see the orange flesh of the pumpkin expand again with a renewed growth spurt. Few people believed him when he told them that at the height of its growth, an Atlantic Giant could gain as much as 12 pounds in flesh every day.

Something you would only believe once you saw it for yourself.

As he drove from farm stall to farm stall selling his pumpkins, he couldn't help but wonder where Hannah had been taking her pumpkins. He hadn't once run into her at a farm stall again. Deep down, he secretly feared that she was withholding all her pumpkins for the fair. Joseph had done the same one year, but only once he had been certain that the grand prize would be his and that the resulting sales would be high.

When he arrived home, he found a note from Mr. Slaghaus on the front door. Joseph glanced around to see who might have put it there, but there was no one in sight. It wasn't the first time a note had been stuck to his door. Since their community's only way of outside communication was the phone shanty, many times someone would call and leave a message.

Whoever answered the phone would make sure they delivered the message.

In his time, Joseph had also stuck notes to doors in the past.

He read the note, and a smile curved his mouth. His wagon was empty, his entire weekly harvest sold, but the note revealed that Mr. Slaghaus needed more pumpkins tomorrow after a school had stopped by and bought all his stock for decorations for a school play.

For a moment, Joseph considered harvesting a few more to deliver tomorrow, when he remembered why he hadn't harvested more. Instead, he headed back to his wagon and called to his horse. "Step up, Simon."

Joseph steered the horse towards the Yoder farm. It had been years since he'd actually set foot on their farm. From the road, you could only see a third of their pumpkin fields. Joseph couldn't help but feel a little curious to see how well Hannah's attempts at becoming a pumpkin farmer were going.

As he pulled up in front of the barn, he couldn't help but feel jealous at the size of her Giant Atlantic's. She had planted the vines just a short distance from the house, no doubt to keep a close eye on her prize winners. Although Joseph wouldn't admit it, her Atlantic Giants looked amazing.

"I'm coming!" her voice came from inside the barn. "You're early!"

Joseph climbed out of his wagon and leaned against it. He crossed his arms and waited for Hannah to appear. At the sight of him, her eyes widened with surprise. "It's you?"

"Jah, expecting someone else?" Joseph asked. For a moment, he felt a little jealous, wondering if she had expected her sweetheart instead of her nemesis.

'Jah, my friend Isabel," Hannah explained, looking a little confused. "What are you doing here? Wait, did my advice work?"

Joseph chuckled. "Jah. I must admit, though, I thought you were trying to sabotage me. But when |I got home and tested the soil for moisture, it was clear you were right. The vines are looking much better and the leaves growing at a gut speed now."

"I'm happy to hear that," Hannah said with a smile that made his heart skip a beat. "But I'm sure you didn't stop by to tell me that. Come to spy on my pumpkins? I can give you a tour if you'd like?"

Joseph felt horrible knowing that was what she thought of him. But then, he couldn't really blame her after the way he had acted towards her before. "Nee, nee. Not at all. I'm not sure if you're selling at the moment, but Mr. Slaghaus needs more pumpkins. He's already sold out, even though I just delivered to him earlier today. I thought perhaps... perhaps you might make a delivery for him tomorrow?"

Hannah's eyes widened with surprise. "Joseph Slaber, are you sharing your vendor with me?"

"I...uh..." Joseph shrugged with a smile. "Like you said, just because we're competing for the same prize doesn't mean we have to be mean."

Hannah's laughter was sweet as it filled the air. Joseph's heart raced even as he felt his chest expand with an unfamiliar feeling. He held her gaze, trying to figure out what it was about her that made him feel this way.

"Denke, Joseph. That's very kind of you."

"It's my pleasure, Hannah." It was the first time he said her name, and it tasted right. Like he was meant to say it many times a day.

Their gazes held, as if neither had anything else to say, but neither of them was willing to say goodbye just yet. When Joseph finally took a step back, he smiled at Hannah with a new kind of hope.

Almost as if he wanted her to succeed. The feeling was as strange as the way his heart raced, and just as unexpected.

"Well, I'll be off then. Gut luck Hannah. Your Giants are looking very gut."

Hannah nodded at him with a smile before she lifted her hand in greeting. Joseph climbed into his wagon and took the reins.

He wasn't sure what had just happened between him and his biggest competitor, but he knew he had experienced nothing like it before.

Chapter 14
Honesty or Treachery

When Hannah arrived home, Isabel was waiting on her porch with a delivery of freshly baked bread.

"This is a gut surprise," Hannah said as she walked up the porch.

"Mamm sent me. She insists you're not eating right. She says if you keep working like you are, you're going to blow away before next spring," Isabel said with a fond smile.

Ever since Hannah's parents had passed away, Isabel's parents had taken it upon themselves to keep an eye on her. Hannah appreciated their concern. "There is nothing as gut as your mamm's bread, denke."

"Besides, it gave me a chance to come and see how your Atlantic Giants are doing. They're big, Hannah!" Isabel said excitedly.

"Jah, I'm hoping they'll grow more now that I've added potassium and more fertilizer," Hannah explained.

Isabel laughed. "I truly appreciate that you're trying to explain to me, but I don't even know what potassium is. Before you even consider explaining, I'm not interested."

Hannah couldn't help but laugh at her friend's honesty. "Then I won't."

"I saw you took the wagon? Another delivery?" Isabel asked as Hannah offered her a glass of homemade iced tea.

"Jah. A very unexpected one, to be honest. Joseph stopped by earlier and asked me to make a delivery to a farm stall he had claimed as his vendor." Hannah shook her head, still baffled by his visit.

"Joseph stopped by… here?" Isabel asked, surprised.

Hannah nodded. "Jah, I was just as surprised."

"You poor thing. Are you sure it wasn't a trap of some sort?" Isabel asked suspiciously.

"Nee, it wasn't. His vendor asked for an extra delivery and Joseph asked me to take it." Hannah shrugged. "But that wasn't the strangest part of his visit…"

"I thought he stopped by. Now it was a visit?" Isabel's eyes widened with curiosity.

"Nee, that's not what I meant. It's just… he was nice. Kind even. It wasn't like the other times I saw him. There was no competition or arrogance, instead it was just…"

"Nice?" Isabel shook her head. "There is definitely something going on. Why would Joseph suddenly be nice to the enemy? You'd better watch your back, Hannah, before he stabs a dagger into it."

"Nee!" Hannah argued. "He wasn't overly sweet or kind, just the usual kind. You remember when you told me how you felt when Daniel looked at you for the first time? Well, don't laugh at me, but for a moment today… that's how I felt," Hannah admitted shyly.

Isabel's eyes softened. "You had a moment with Joseph Slaber?"

"I think so. I've experienced nothing like it before. It was as if everything disappeared into the background, and it was just... us."

"How do you know he didn't fabricate the visit and the moment just to soften you up so he could take the prize?"

"I don't. That's why I'm confused. How will I know if it really was *something* and if he was just trying to fool me?" Hannah asked, feeling out of her element.

Isabel's mouth curved into a smile. "Easy. The quickest way to see if someone is really interested in you or just playing with you is to test them. Since you and Joseph are both competing for the prize at the fair, I'd say test his intentions."

"How would I do that?" Hannah asked, shaking her head.

"Easy. Pay him a visit... then ask him for advice. Ask him about something you know the answer to. If he gives you the wrong advice, you'll know he is just trying to soften you up to win the prize. If he gives you the right advice... then I'm afraid to say you had a moment with the enemy."

"We're not enemies!" Hannah insisted.

"Perhaps not, but you are competitors," Isabel reminded her. "If there was a connection between you, Hannah, what are you going to do about it? Someone is going to win at the fair and it doesn't matter who wins, the other person is going to feel thwarted."

"Not if it's an honest win." Hannah insisted. "I'll do what you say. I'll ask him for advice. At least that will help me make sense of the moment we had. If it even was that..."

Isabel smiled broadly. "You don't experience something like that every day. If you had a moment, you'd know it."

Hannah nodded. If she went by what Isabel was saying, then she in fact shared a moment with Joseph Slaber.

Chapter 15
Marigolds & Mystery

A few days after Joseph had stopped by Hannah's place, he was still thinking about her as he inspected his vines.

The last thing he'd expected was to feel attracted to her. He had never been interested in courtship, instead believing in God's promise that love will find him. And as he stood in front of Hannah, he had wondered if God's promise had come true.

For the first time in his life, he had looked at a woman with more than a passing interest. When he had looked into Hannah's eyes, he had felt something he had never felt before: curiosity.

In the past, he would appreciate a woman's beauty, he would even appreciate her conversation, but never had he been curious about a woman. About what made her smile, what made her cry, and how he could make her laugh.

He was curious about her determination and work ethic. He was curious about her independence—did she enjoy it? And more than anything, he was curious about the way his heart had swelled in his chest when she had smiled at him.

Row for row, Joseph walked through his vines. At this stage in the growth process, the vines were susceptible to squash beetles. It was something that you would miss one day and the next it could attack your entire crop.

First, he had checked his prize vines before he continued into the fields of jack-o'-lanterns. A smile curved his mouth as he wondered if Hannah would do the same. He couldn't help but be surprised at her knowledge. For someone that was bringing in their first harvest, she seemed more than capable and knowledgeable enough to do so.

Joseph turned and started down the next row when he noticed someone to waving to him from the barn. His heart skipped a beat the moment he recognized Hannah's smile. It was as if his thoughts had conjured her in his yard.

He blinked a few times and looked again. And yet, Hannah stood in front of his barn with a wide smile. "Hullo!"

Joseph felt his mouth curve into a smile as he waved back. His pace quickened as he rushed towards the barn, eager to see her again. He wasn't supposed to want to spend time with her or even talk to her; instead, he should keep his distance like he used to do with her father. But there was something about Hannah that drew him like a magnet.

"Hullo," Joseph greeted her as he reached the barn. "Kumm to give me some more advice?"

Hannah laughed and shook her head. "Nee, not at all. Doesn't seem like you need it. Your fields are in great condition."

"So are my Giant Atlantic's, thanks to you," Joseph said with a hesitant smile. Why did he feel foolish and excited at the same time?

"I was hoping you might return the favor, actually?" Hannah asked hopefully. "I spotted a squash beetle on the leaf of jack-o'-lantern yesterday, and this morning it seems as if he has invited his whole family and distant relatives to my field," Hannah sighed, shaking her head.

"I'm sorry to hear that," Joseph sympathized. Hannah might be the competition, but Joseph didn't wish that pest on his worst enemy.

"Jah, me too," Hannah said, shaking her head. "The thing is, from what I've read, the best option is to spray them with a diluted solution of water and dishwashing liquid. I've also read about gut pesticides, but I don't want to ruin my harvest with chemicals."

"The price falls quite a lot once you use pesticides," Joseph nodded in agreement. "Do you have nasturtiums between your vines?"

"Jah?" Hannah said, looking confused. "I tried to weed them out, but they keep coming up. Daed used to plant them everywhere. Perhaps they looked pretty to him. Do they attract the squash beetle?"

Joseph smiled, feeling grateful that there was something that he could help her with. If it hadn't been for her advice, he might not have saved his Atlantic Giants. "Your daed planted them because they deter squash beetles. try to get some more nasturtiums and plant them everywhere you can find a spot. I've got some Marigolds I'll repot for you, that you can plant as well. Between the marigolds and the nasturtiums, your problem should be solved. As a last measure, especially with your Atlantic Giants, you can sprinkle diatomaceous earth around the base of the vine and your pumpkins."

"Marigolds? I've never heard of Marigolds in a pumpkin field before?" Hannah asked, a little cautious just to accept his advice.

"Marigolds deter not only the squash beetles, but they attract the tachinid fly. The flies prey on the eggs of the beetles. So it's a natural way to alter the ecosystem of your field," Joseph explained.

Hannah's smile brightened. "Denke Joseph. I'll definitely try that."

"Here, let me fetch those marigolds for you. Remember, in the future, when you sow your pumpkins seeds, start germinating nasturtiums and marigolds as well. That way, when you have a problem, they're ready to be planted in the field to do their job." Joseph led her around the barn where he had almost three dozen Marigolds standing in pots.

"Goodness, your marigolds are beautiful," Hannah complimented him.

"Denke. As they're the ambulances of the vines, I take gut care of them," Joseph explained. "You can take them as they are, no need to repot them. Plant them in the ground instead of just lacing the pots around your field."

Hannah shook her head with a curious smile. "Denke Joseph. I didn't know what I was expecting, but I wasn't expecting such kindness from you."

Joseph shrugged, feeling a little shy. "You started it."

They shared a laugh before their gazes met and locked. Again, there it was, Joseph thought as he searched Hannah's gaze. That connection and curiosity made him search her gaze as if he would find the answers there.

Something about Hannah made him want to get to know her better.

A light blush colored her cheeks as she glanced away. "I've got to get going. Take the ambulances home."

Joseph chuckled. "Jah, the sooner you get rid of those beetles, the better. Would you like me to come and help?"

Hannah quickly shook her head. "Nee, I'm sure I'll be fine. Let me know what I owe you for the marigolds?"

"Nothing. A gift from one farmer to another," Joseph said with a warm smile.

He helped her load up the marigolds and watched her drive away. As she became smaller in the distance, Joseph took off his hat and dragged a hand through his hair.

Why did he have a feeling that Hannah was going to do much more than offer him competition at the fall fair?

She might just steal the prize and take his heart with it.

Chapter 16
Height x Weight = Love

The year was coming to an end.

As Hannah walked with her tape measure in hand towards her Atlantic Giants, the thought struck her like a bolt of lightning.

Next week it would be the pumpkin fair, then it would be Thanksgiving a few weeks later, and before she knew it, it would be Christmas.

Her throat constricted with emotion as she realized it would be her first Thanksgiving and Christmas alone. A tear slipped over her cheek at the memory of holidays past. Her mother would cook turkey, pumpkin pie, potatoes, and the most amazing stuffing every Thanksgiving.

They would sit around the dinner table and give thanks for all their blessings. Not only the blessings of the last year, but the blessings of family and love as well. Another tear joined the first, as Hannah realized how little she had to be thankful for this year.

She had lost her parents and would spend Thanksgiving alone. Would she give thanks for the loss, for the hardships it had caused, or for the loneliness she experienced every day?

As she neared the Atlantic Giants, Hannah swallowed back the tears and reminded herself she had a lot to be grateful for. She could give thanks for the knowledge she had gained about pumpkin farming over the last few months. She could give thanks for her bountiful harvest, and she could also give thanks that Joseph had passed her test.

The advice he had given her resounded with her father's notes on pest control. Although she didn't really have need for the marigolds, planting them had made her happy. Every time she walked through her fields, she thought of Joseph when she saw them.

She had picked out three Atlantic Giants a week ago. They were to be her competitors for the grand prize. Today she would measure them and calculate their weight. With great care, she measured the pumpkins. One didn't appear bigger than the others, but when measured, it was two inches wider than the others and an inch taller.

We have a winner on our hands, Hannah thought with a hopeful smile. But as she spotted a marigold, she felt a little anxious about what Joseph's pumpkins would yield.

This was her first year trying to grow a giant pumpkin. Joseph had been doing it for years. She might believe that her pumpkins were prize winners, but then she did not know the size of Joseph's pumpkins.

She pushed thoughts of Christmas and Thanksgiving aside and made a silent vow to focus all her energy on the grand prize at the fair.

That would give her the ultimate blessing to be thankful for on Thanksgiving.

***

Joseph's father didn't believe in measuring his pumpkins. Instead, he would wait until the day before the fair and then measure which pumpkin to enter the Giant Pumpkin competition.

In every other aspect of farming, Joseph did things the way his father did. Except when it came to measuring pumpkins. Nothing was more rewarding for Joseph than to measure his pumpkins a week before the fair.

Not only did the overnight growth surprise him every single morning, but it built the excitement for the day of the competition. For Joseph, it was an exciting way to end the season of growing and harvesting pumpkins.

As he pulled out the tape measure and measured the Atlantic Giant's, a smile curved his mouth. He had one giant that would definitely outweigh his entry from the year before. Hope surged through his veins at the thought of the grand prize.

Not only would it give him enough money to fertilize all his fields properly before the next growing season, but it would also allow him to open a savings account to save for unexpected events. Joseph didn't mind living from hand to mouth, but he was a man and needed to think about his future.

When he had a family one day, Joseph needed to be able to provide for them should something happen to his harvest. He knew it was a distant dream, but that didn't mean he couldn't plan for it now. Even as soon as the thought occurred to him, it brought Hannah's visit to his mind.

He smiles as he remembered. It had been the best surprise ever to see Hannah waiting for him in front of his barn. Even better than he could've imagined it would be. But the best part about her visit was that she had come to him for advice.

Of course, Joseph could've sabotaged her, like he had planned to do a couple of months ago, but he found him wanting to help her. Regardless that she was the competition, Joseph wanted her to succeed. No one knew better than Joseph how much work and prayer went into growing pumpkins. There was nothing worse than having squash beetles take that from you.

For a moment, he considered paying her a visit to find out if she had won the war against the beetles.

He shook his head as he tucked the tape measure back into his pocket. Although he wanted nothing more than to see Hannah again, he didn't want to be too forward. The competition was only a week away and when he won the grand prize, he didn't want her to feel belittled. Joseph wanted to make sure that she knew that what she had achieved was amazing.

Especially considering it's her first year as a pumpkin farmer.

He smiled again as he walked back to the barn. Was it wrong of him to look forward to the fall fair?

Not because it would give him the opportunity to do the final sales push for the season, but because it meant he would see Hannah every day.

Chapter 17
Competition Day

"Oh my goodness, Hannah!" Isabel clapped her hands together with excitement. "Can you believe you grew that monster all by yourself?"

Hannah laughed and shook her head. "Not at all."

It was the day before the fall fair started. The day of the final weigh in for everyone who wanted to compete in the Giant Pumpkin competition. Hannah had coffee waiting just after dawn, as her friends and neighbors helped her move her biggest pumpkin onto the wagon.

The wagon had creaked beneath the weight, and for a moment Hannah had been concerned it wouldn't be able to carry her large pumpkin to the fair. But with Isabel's beau, Daniel, behind the reins, her pumpkin had arrived safely at its destination.

The lineup of pumpkins stood impressively side by side. Every farmer standing beside their entry waiting for it to be judged on color and health before it was measured.

For the first time, Hannah realized why her father had enjoyed growing giant pumpkins. It wasn't only because of the challenge and the art it required, but it was for this moment.

Standing beside a giant pumpkin made you feel as if you achieved something thousands couldn't. It made her feel strong and confident in ways she had never experienced before. What made her feel even more confident with her capabilities was that she was the only woman amongst a group of fifteen men. Some competitors had come over to introduce themselves, while others had simply given her a wary look from afar.

Many recognized Hannah as her father's daughter and sympathized with her loss. But Hannah knew that their sympathy wouldn't let her win. The only thing that stood between her and the grand prize was her pumpkin.

The judged had moved all the way down the line and now stood and deliberated on one end. Hannah took the time to inspect the pumpkin line up herself, as most of the farmers did while they waited.

When the judges returned, everyone fell back into line.

Hannah anxiously waited as the head judge stepped forward.

"Congratulations to every single one of you. This must be the best lineup of Giant Pumpkins we've had in years. To have a pumpkin reach this size requires not only determination and skill, but dedication and a lot of hard work. You can pat yourselves on the back for that."

Hannah smiled down the line of competitors when she found Joseph looking her way. He mouthed the words *good luck,* and Hannah did the same.

"Unfortunately, for most of you, the road ends here. To reward you for your participation this year, you will receive a 15% discount on any pumpkin seed brought from the co-op for next year's planting season. You can collect your vouchers with my colleague when I read your name."

Hannah drew in a deep breath as names were read. Every time the judge spoke, she feared he would read her name next.

"Thank you once again to all of you for participating. Our final two in the running for the grand prize for the Giant Pumpkin competition is Joseph Slaber and Hannah Yoder."

Applause sounded through the air as Hannah turned to Joseph with a wide-eyed look of surprise. Of course, she had hoped to win the grand prize, but deep down she had doubted to even make it this far into the competition at all.

"The final weigh in will take place after lunch. That means we can return to the scales in two hours' time. Joseph, Hannah, good luck."

Hannah let go of the breath she had held. Laughter bubbled from her throat with relief when Isabel came rushing towards her. "You did it! You're in the final weigh in."

Hannah nodded. "I know. I can hardly believe it. Our pumpkin, though... it looks just about the same size."

"Only weight will tell," Joseph said, joining them. "I was going to grab something to eat at the diner. I was wondering if you'd like to join me—before you never speak to me again for snatching away the grand prize."

Hannah couldn't help but smile. "You mean before you never speak to me again?"

Joseph chuckled. "Either way, care to join me?"

Hannah glanced at Isabel, who simply held up her hands. "I just remembered I have an errand to run." Isabel disappeared into the crowd of people.

Hannah turned back to Joseph and hesitated for a moment before she followed her heart. Her mind warned her that becoming friends with her biggest competitor might not be the wisest thing to do, but her heart begged her to spend a little more time with Joseph.

"Alright, I'll join you for lunch, Joseph," Hannah smiled at him with a challenge in her eyes.

"Wunderbaar. Perhaps I can sneak some poison into your food, then I'll win by default."

Hannah laughed. "Perhaps I've already thought of that."

Feeling happy and enjoying the banter, Hannah fell into step beside Joseph as they walked towards the diner.

Chapter 18
Follow Your Heart

Joseph hadn't planned on asking Hannah for lunch.

The moment the judge announced that one of them was the winner, he might lose his chance. Joseph knew that if he wanted to explore the attraction between them, he needed to do it before the weigh in. He was kidding when he said she wouldn't ever speak to him again, but secretly he feared that was what would happen.

Sitting across from her in the diner, Joseph felt more drawn to her than ever before. He could see that she was just as anxiously excited as he was to learn who had won the grand prize.

"How is your food?" Joseph asked when she pushed her empty plate forward.

Hannah chuckled and shook her head. "Evidently I'm a nervous eater. It was delicious. If that's what poison tastes like, I'd like some more."

Joseph laughed. "Luckily, I'm too honest to poison you. Although I fear you might beat me at the weigh in."

"I don't think you have anything to fear. With measurements, yours is slightly bigger..." Hannah trailed off with a shrug.

Joseph searched her gaze and smiled at her with warmth in his gaze. "Will you forgive me if I win?"

Hannah nodded. "Of course I will. Although there is nothing to forgive. I think with growing giant pumpkins, a lot of it comes down to knowledge and hard work, but there is an element of luck as well."

Joseph chuckled. "That's what I always thought."

"See, great minds think alike," Hannah commented with a smile.

Joseph glanced at the time on his pocket watch and sighed heavily. "I wish we didn't have to go back just yet."

"Is it already time?"

Joseph nodded. "Just about. Before we go, Hannah, I want to tell you I underestimated you. When your parents passed away…. I honestly thought you'd sell the farm and move in with relatives. After learning that you were planning on growing your own harvest, I laughed. I know it was terrible of me, but I just couldn't imagine a girl, a woman, growing an entire pumpkin harvest by herself. I'm proud of what you achieved this year Hannah, I'm even prouder to know someone so kind and determined. You make a great pumpkin farmer."

Hannah's eyes welled up slightly as she laughed softly. "Wow, I wasn't expecting that. Especially not from you."

Joseph shrugged. "Perhaps you should expect the unexpected."

When Hannah smiled at him in that way that made his breath catch and his heart skip a beat, Joseph knew he wouldn't forgive himself if he won the grand prize. For him, it meant continuing his father's legacy, but for Hannah it would mean so much more.

Sure, Joseph needed the money if he wanted to fertilize his fields, but it wasn't just about the money anymore. Hannah was the real winner. Regardless of her grief and the challenges she had faced this year, she had grown a bountiful harvest and had surprised him with not only her kindness in offering him advice but also her talent for growing giant pumpkins.

"Denke Joseph," Hannah said, standing up.

Joseph reached for her hand and held her gaze. When he looked into her eyes, it was almost as if he had stepped out of the shadows and into the light. As if the light was suddenly shining on a bright future. "Just one more thing, Hannah... your daed would've been very proud."

Hannah smiled at him gratefully. "I think he would've been proud of you, too. For helping me with the beetles."

Joseph nodded. "It was the least I could do."

Together they walked back to the fair grounds. When they arrived, a crowd had already gathered. Their pumpkins had been hoisted onto giant scales, the digital displays not yet switched on.

Joseph looked at the pumpkins side by side, and knew that he was going to do the right thing. It might be something his father wouldn't have agreed with, but Joseph knew he wouldn't forgive himself otherwise.

"Excuse me," Joseph said to Hannah before he made his way to the judges.

A few moments later, the judges gathered in front of the scales and called Hannah closer. The same man as before addressed the crowd.

"Ladies and Gentlemen we have a winner. Mr. Joseph Slaber has retracted his entry to the competition this year for personal reasons. That means that by default, Miss Hannah Yoder is the winner of this year's grand prize."

Joseph watched as Hannah's eyes widened with joy. That moment made losing the prize money and the best stand at the fair worth it. But then a frown creased her brow as she shook her head adamantly.

Chapter 19
Her Daed's Dochder

"Nee, I can't just win by default. You need to do the weigh in," Hannah insisted, loud enough for everyone to year.

Joseph walked to her and took both her her hands in his. "Hannah, I don't care about the weight or the competition. You deserve the win. You've accomplished more in a few months than most pumpkin farmers achieve during their entire lives."

"I don't care, Joseph. I won't take the prize by default. Otherwise, I'm withdrawing my entry as well and someone else will win."

Joseph shook his head. "Hannah, don't be ferhoodled. You can't let one of them have the prize. If I agree to the weigh in, promise me you'll keep the prize."

"Fair is fair, Joseph. I appreciate the offer, but I'd rather find out whose pumpkin is the biggest." Hannah jutted out her chin stubbornly.

Hannah wasn't sure why Joseph had withdrawn himself from the competition, but she hadn't spent the last few weeks checking on her pumpkins many times a day just to win the prize by default.

She needed to know the weight, not only for herself, but to prove to the other farmers that she was going to continue with her farm. Joseph had complimented her at the diner and even now she couldn't help but feel proud of herself. In the past, Joseph and her father had always fought over vendors, racing to sell their pumpkins first.

Not only had Hannah acquired the skill and the knowledge to grow pumpkins in such a short time, but she had also found a new sales avenue for herself. She had learned to put in irrigation, and she had learned about marigolds and nasturtiums. Some might think that if she won by default, it was out of sympathy for her father, who wasn't standing there himself this year.

She couldn't build her future on sympathy.

"Hannah, it doesn't matter," Joseph insisted.

She shook her head. "It matters, Joseph, it matters to me."

The judge, who had spoken a few seconds before, glanced first at Joseph before he turned to Hannah. "Joseph, does that mean you're back in the competition?"

Before Joseph could answer, Hannah nodded. "Jah, he's back. We'd like to find out the final weights now, please."

The judge turned to Joseph with a questioning look. "I need to hear it from you?"

Joseph shook his head. "I don't care how much the pumpkins weigh. She deserves to be the winner. This was her first harvest, her first year even growing an Atlantic Giant…"

"Joseph, don't be ferhoodled. You've worked for this just as hard as I have. You're not thinking this through. If you withdraw now and your pumpkin is the winner, you're losing the prime spot at the fall fair. My daed often told me what a difference having the prime spot makes in selling jack-o'-lanterns." Hannah was insistent, stubborn almost, but Joseph could be stubborn as well.

"Like I said, I don't care about the weight," Joseph repeated.

"Folks, we need to finalize who the winner is," the judge reminded them.

Hannah turned to Joseph with a pleading look. "Joseph, I need this. If I win, I want it to be because my pumpkin won, not because you pity me for everything I've faced this year. Please, don't let me hang my head in shame because everyone doubts I was the true winner."

Hannah saw Joseph's expression change to one of anger. "I'm not doing it because I pity you. But if you really feel that strongly about it," Joseph turned to the judge. "I'm back in the competition."

The judge's smile split his face in two. "Wonderful. Gather round, gather round. It's time for the moment we've all been waiting for!"

People moved closer, clearly everyone having their own suspicion about who the winner was going to be.

"Every year, for the last seventy-five years, our town has celebrated the fall fair. Not only is it a harvest festival for farmers all around, but it gives our pumpkin farms the opportunity to take part in the biggest competition in the state. The Giant Pumpkin competition."

Hannah took deep slow breaths as she listened to the judge tell everyone about the history of the competition and how Howard Dill had grown the first Atlantic Giant pumpkin. By the time he thoroughly informed the crowd about the importance and achievement this competition held, everyone was anxiously waiting for the winner to be announced.

"Before we switch on the scales, there is one last thing we want to share with you. Although these farmers grew their giant pumpkins, they won't be taking them home. One condition of entering the giant pumpkin competition is that we would donate all giant pumpkins to charities in and around our county. Each pumpkin can feed many hungry bellies, so not only is it an achievement to grow one, but it's a charitable endeavor as well."

"Weigh in! Weigh in! The crowd began to chant.

Hannah glanced at Joseph with a hopeful smile. Before she knew it, Joseph walked towards her and took her hand in his. "Gut luck, Hannah."

His hand was warm and large as it held hers. It made a shiver run up her arm. "You too."

As the crowd continued to chant, the judge announced the scales were to be switched on.

Hannah looked at Joseph and he held her gaze. The crowd shouted with excitement, but Hannah couldn't dare drag her eyes away from Joseph. Just like he had said a few moments before, the weights didn't matter. Here, between them, she felt something ignite that mattered much more.

"Hannah! Look up!" Isabel cried out as she rushed towards her. "You won! Your pumpkin won!"

Hannah's jaw dropped with surprise even as Daniel stepped in front of them. "Barely. When it comes to Giant Pumpkins, four pounds is barely a difference."

Joseph shook his head, still holding Hannah's gaze. "Four pounds makes Hannah the winner of the grand prize."

"Daniel is right. It's such a negligible difference. I'd like the share the prize money with you," Hannah only felt it was right.

Joseph laughed and shook his head. "Nee, denke, but nee. You keep that prize money and you're going to have the best stand at the fair. Congratulations Hannah! You did it."

He squeezed her hand tightly, and Hannah felt her heart skip a beat.

Isabel tugged away from Joseph and pointed up to the screens where the digital scale readings were still up on display. She couldn't help but be surprised to see that her pumpkin weighed in at just over eight hundred pounds. Tears flooded her eyes as she realized she hadn't only won the grand prize at the fair, but she had exceeded her father's best weight.

It was wonderful to know that regardless of all the challenges she had faced, she followed her in father's footsteps.

And he would've been proud.

Chapter 20
Feeding the Opposition

Joseph didn't pout about the weight of Hannah's pumpkin, instead, he celebrated her win. When he had taken her out to lunch, he had realized that Hannah meant more to him than just being his competition.

That was why, instead of glancing at all the customers at her stall with envy, he smiled every time he saw how excited she was about selling another pumpkin. Joseph could watch her selling pumpkins for the rest of his life and he wouldn't have a single complaint, he thought, as she sold yet another pumpkin.

It was the third day of the fair; Halloween was only two days away. Joseph knew that if the fair was brimming with people now, it would only be busier tomorrow, and even busier on the last day. He hurried to the lady that owned the stall beside him and asked her to keep an eye on his stall for a little while.

On the first day of the fair, Joseph had walked over to ask Hannah if she was managing, although it was clear that she was. Yesterday, his excuse to spend time with her had been to ask her about her harvest and if she needed help, which she didn't.

Joseph had never thought up excuses to talk to a woman, but with Hannah, he felt foolish just walking up to her. Although they had the competition behind them, it still felt as if they shouldn't be friends. As if there was a line drawn in the sand between the two biggest pumpkin farmers in the community.

Whilst selling pumpkins during the morning, he had thought up a different excuse for today. Luckily, fate had played him a good hand, and just like he had hoped, Hannah couldn't seem to get a minute to escape from her stall for something to drink or to eat.

As her stall was the one from the entrance, most people that just needed pumpkins bought their pumpkins from her instead of moving in further and comparing prices. It was the stall Joseph had hoped for, but now was glad he didn't have.

Just like winning the grand prize, Hannah deserved to sell her entire harvest. Without needing to compete with Hannah when he sold to his farm stalls and vendors, Joseph had already made a better profit from the year before. He might not fertilize all his fields, but he would at least be able to fertilize at least half of his farm properly.

Joseph bought two corn dogs and two sodas before he found his way back to Hannah's stall.

"Denke, happy carving!" Hannah waved to a client that had just bought eight pumpkins for Halloween. As they pushed their cart back to their car, Joseph stood by and watched with a smile.

Only when Hannah turned around did she notice him standing there. "Joseph, I almost sold you a pumpkin."

"You probably would've managed to. It seems you have a knack for selling." Joseph offered her the corn dog and soda. "Here, I noticed you've been too busy to escape for a few minutes."

"Denke, it's very kind of you. I'm starving," Hannah admitted, taking a bite of her corn dog.

"My pleasure. Think you'll have enough pumpkins for the next two days? The way you're selling, I'd think you're nearly out," Joseph asked.

Hannah shrugged. "Time will tell. I still have some on the vines at home. I might have to harvest through the night if it comes to that." Her laughter made his heart swell.

Why was it that the more time he spent with Hannah, the more time he wanted to spend with her? "Just let me know if you need help. I've been known to have gut vision at night."

Hannah's brow lifted. "Cat-like eyes… that's curious."

"Not as curious as my strength," Joseph teased. "I've carried a few pumpkins in my time."

His teasing made her laugh again. "You sound like quite the farmer."

"Just like you," Joseph complimented her.

"Hold onto this please." Hannah handed him her corn dog as more clients arrived. Joseph watched as she asked them all kinds of questions. After making herself familiar with her clients and what they would use the pumpkins for, she sold them three instead of the one they had come for.

"That is a talent, I've yet to learn," Joseph said as she reached again for her corn dog.

Hannah shrugged. "It doesn't help if I sell them pie pumpkins when they would do better with a cheaper carving pumpkin."

"But they're all jack-o'-lanterns?" Joseph asked, confused.

Hannah nodded. "They are, but I've separated them. Over there are the ones with the best flesh, although their skin might be a little bleached by the sun. Here, you have the ones I've set aside for carving. They're shaped perfectly and their skin is a glossy orange."

"Once again, I learn from the novice. Hannah Yoder, you truly are everything I didn't expect," Joseph mused at her salesmanship.

"Just like you are much kinder than I thought. Do you know that when you jumped in front of my wagon that day at the farm stall, I was certain you were going to unleash a pest on my vines, or try to sabotage my wagon?" Hannah laughed, shaking her head.

Joseph swallowed past the guilty lump in his throat. "I might have considered it, but now that I've come to know you… I would never do something like that."

"Gut to know." Hannah smiled at him. "I really enjoy talking to you, Joseph."

Joseph felt his heart skip a beat with hope as he flashed her a full wattage smile. "I really like talking to you, too."

Joseph wouldn't say that his future with Hannah was as good as planned, but he had a feeling that the likelihood was growing every day.

Chapter 21
A Curious Question

The following afternoon, Hannah couldn't help but be grateful that the next day would be the last of the fair. They had blessed her with exceptional sales this week and along with the grand prize money, she knew she didn't have to worry about losing the family farm.

But she was exhausted, mentally and physically.

Now that the pumpkin season had ended she realized how hard she had worked over the last few months. Spending the last three days selling pumpkins all day had tired her even more. When she wasn't standing, she was carrying pumpkins. Her back was sore and her hands were calloused, but her bank account was smiling.

After closing up her stall for the day, she counted how many pumpkins she had left. She only had thirty-five pumpkins, which would sell before the day was over tomorrow. A smile curved her mouth as she walked to where her buggy was, as she thought about Joseph's offer to come and help her harvest at night.

The last person she had expected to befriend after losing her parents was her father's greatest competition. And yet Joseph had proven over and over again to her what a kind and generous person he was. When he had brought her the corn dog and soda the day before, she had nearly wept with relief. She hadn't realized how busy her stall would be when she won the prize.

But now she knew many customers didn't visit the fair itself. They only came for the pumpkins. Which meant instead of perusing all the different arts, crafts, and home-made goods, they barely crossed the entrance of the fair to buy their pumpkins from her before they went on their way.

Hannah set down her purse in the buggy before she collected her horse from the stables, where the fair allowed their horses to stay during the day. Just as she reached the stables, she saw Joseph waiting for her with a smile.

"Hullo Joseph," Hannah greeted him with a smile in return. She hadn't even had time to return the favor by buying him lunch today.

"Hullo Hannah," Joseph smiled at her with a sparkle in his eyes. "I was wondering if you would like to go for a ride?"

"A ride?" Hannah asked, confused, before she shook her head. "Is there something wrong with my horse?"

Hannah moved towards the stable and peered inside, only to see her horse was as fit as he was when she had left him that morning.

"Nee, nee," Joseph shook his head, almost shuffling in place. "The horse is fine. I just thought I'd offer."

"Denke, but we're fine." Hannah took her horse out of the stable and smiled at Joseph one last time. "Have a gut evening."

"You too," Joseph said, sounding strange.

Hannah wasn't sure what was going on with him or why he was acting so strange. Once she had her horse hitched to the buggy, she headed towards Isabel's home. Isabel's parents had invited Hannah for dinner tonight, and instead of going home first, Hannah planned on heading straight there.

It was part of Isabel's mother's plan to fatten Hannah up after she had lost so much weight. But with the long hours Hannah had put in at the fair this week, she was more than grateful that she didn't have to cook.

As always, Isabel's parents were kind and caring. They asked her how the fair was going and if she needed any help on the farm. Isabel's mother asked about Hannah's health, while her father offered to come and chop wood for Hannah before the winter arrived.

By the time dinner was over and Hannah was on her way home, Isabel walked her out. "I swear, sometimes they love you more than they love me."

Hannah laughed. "You're imaging in things. Denke for dinner, it was truly wunderbaar."

"You're always welcome. I wanted to ask you… you mentioned the moment with Joseph before the fair. Has something similar happened again?"

Hannah stopped and thought for a moment. "I'm not sure. He's been really friendly. We've talked every day at the fair." A blush covered her cheeks. "Jah, we had another moment, but that was before this afternoon."

"What happened this afternoon?" Isabel asked curiously.

"I'm not sure. He offered me a ride? I don't know why he would do something like that when I had my horse and my buggy there. When I declined politely, he acted strange." Hannah shrugged. "I'm not sure if I offended him?"

Isabel's eyes widened as she tried to stop herself from laughing. "You told him your horse and buggy were fine?"

"Jah, more or less. What's so funny?" Hannah asked, too tired to guess.

Isabel burst out laughing and shook her head. "Hannah, he wasn't asking you if your horse was ill or if your buggy had a broken wheel. Joseph was trying to ask you on a buggy ride. A real buggy ride."

Hannah's eyes widened with surprise. "Really? Are you sure? I don't think he would ask me on a real buggy ride."

"He was willing to hand you the grand prize, Hannah. He's brought you lunch and found excuses to come over and talk to you. You forget, Daniel tells me everything he learns from Joseph. Joseph is trying his best to court you, and you're too naïve to even notice it."

"Why would he want to court me?" Hannah asked, surprised.

"Because he likes you, you ferhoodled fool. Now go home and get a gut night's sleep. Then tomorrow, make sure you let him know you like him as well. Before long it's the holidays and then everyone is so consumed with everything Christmas, and spending time with family, that your opportunity might have passed." Isabel flinched and shook her head. "I'm sorry Hannah, I didn't mean to remind you about your familye."

"It's all right. I understood," Hannah consoled her. "Although I do not know how to do that."

"You'll figure out. By the way, mamm asks if you eat pear stuffing. She's planning on making some for-Thanksgiving dinner."

Hannah had thought about Thanksgiving a few times over the last week. She appreciated her friend's invitation, but Isabel was right. Thanksgiving was time for family. "I eat pear stuffing, but I won't be coming Isabel. Please apologize to your mamm for me. I know you might not understand it, but I don't want to intrude."

Isabel held her gaze for a moment, ready to argue, before she finally nodded. "I'll explain to Mamm. But if you change your mind at the last minute, you're welcome."

"Denke."

As Hannah drove home in the darkness, she thought of Joseph again. Did he truly ask her on a buggy ride and she hadn't even realized it?

Chapter 22
A Beginning & An End

It had taken Joseph all day to gather enough courage to ask Hannah to go on a buggy ride with him. When she'd so easily turned him down, he couldn't help but wonder if he was the only one to feel the attraction between them.

He had spent the night tossing and turning, barely catching a wink of sleep at all. The more he thought about Hannah, the more he doubted if he had made his intentions clear when he'd asked her to go on a buggy ride.

Since hadn't ever done it before, he couldn't help but feel humiliated because she had turned him down so easily.

Now that it was the last day of the fair, Joseph had decided that today would be his last chance to learn if Hannah really liked him, or if she was just being friendly the way she was with everyone else.

But Joseph didn't want to be anyone else. He wanted to be her someone special.

He wanted to be as special to her as she was to him.

Joseph arrived early at the fair and spent most of the morning watching Hannah from afar. He tried to figure out what it was about her that attracted him so much. But the more he watched her, the more he realized it wasn't just one thing.

It was everything.

It was her kindness, her friendliness, and her laugh. It was the way she braided her hair, and the way she smiled. It was the way she held herself, with humbleness and pride at the same time. It was the way she allowed herself to be fragile, and yet she was the strongest woman that Joseph had ever met.

He watched as she sold her last pumpkin and felt proud of her for making such a success in her stall. When she walked over to him triumphantly, she was kind enough to look a little sympathetic because he still had over fifty pumpkins left to sell.

"Denke, now that you're all out, hopefully I'll sell some pumpkins," Joseph teased.

Hannah's laughter filled the air as she shook her head. "Joseph, I can't believe I sold all my pumpkins. Now I just have the last field's harvest to deliver on Monday and the season will officially be over."

Joseph nodded. "It's fun, but it's exhausting, isn't it?"

Hannah nodded in agreement. "More exhausting than I realized, but then it's also more rewarding than I could've imagined. Ach Joseph, I feel horrible for saying this has been the best week of my life. Especially because my parents weren't here to share it with me."

Joseph felt his heart clench for her. He could imagine that bittersweet achievement. He'd experienced it the first year after he'd lost his father. "I'm glad you had so much fun, and I'm sure your parents are smiling down at you right now."

"Denke, it helps to hear you say that." Hannah smiled at him warmly and let out a contented sigh. "Do you still have pumpkins on the vine?"

Joseph nodded. "Just my last field, like you. I'll be harvesting and delivering on Monday."

"And then... what do you do for the rest of the month?" Hannah asked curiously.

Joseph chuckled. "I pull out the vines, I burn some of them for the ash and then I start a compost heap. Then, of course, there are all the winter chores..." Joseph trailed off. Today was the last chance he had to talk to Hannah without having to need an excuse to see her. There was one question in particular he wanted to ask. "Hannah, where have you been selling your pumpkins?"

Hannah's mouth curved into a secretive smile. "Really? You haven't figured it out yet?"

Joseph shook his head with a smile. "Nee, I haven't for the life of me."

Hannah laughed softly before she explained. When Joseph listened to the calculations she had made and the deal she had signed with the local grocer, he couldn't help but be even more impressed. Before he realized it, the words tumbled from his mouth. "You truly are an amazing woman, Hannah. An inspiration."

Hannah's cheeks flushed lightly as her eyes shyly turned to the ground. "Denke Joseph."

"Don't thank me. It's the truth. I've never found myself more intrigued or captivated by anything than I am by you." Joseph stopped himself before he scared her off for good. "I just mean... that was real clever of you."

Hannah cleared her throat. "At least we weren't fighting over farm stalls anymore."

Joseph felt a smile curve his mouth. "Perhaps I enjoyed fighting over farm stalls with you."

"I like this more." Hannah's voice had softened, but her words struck home for Joseph.

He hadn't imagined it. Hannah liked him. She just felt a little surprised by it, just like Joseph.

After she left, Joseph felt his heart expand with hope.

The pumpkin season might be over, but his courtship with Hannah was just about to start.

Chapter 23
A Service to Remember

After seeing Joseph every day during the festival, Hannah missed him the following week. She caught herself thinking of him at the most unexpected times.

And every time she did, she wondered what he was doing and if he was thinking about her as well. She had tried her best to show him she liked him on the last day of the fair, but she still didn't know if she had done it right.

Hannah couldn't help but wish that she had followed her mother's advice and had attended Sunday singings sooner. Perhaps if she had watched her friends court and how they acted, she wouldn't have felt as out of her depth or as unsure about how to reveal her feelings to a man.

But then perhaps she wasn't supposed to reveal her feelings, or that she was attracted.

It was too confusing.

A sigh escaped her as she took the reins of her buggy. It was Sunday, and Hannah was looking forward to service more than ever before. Not for the message the deacon would deliver, but for the opportunity to see Joseph again.

With hope in her heart, she called to her horse and headed to the farm where the service was being held today. Ever since her parents had passed away, Sunday service had become a chore for Hannah. She enjoyed the service and listening to Gott's word, but it was the community that exhausted her.

Hannah wasn't sure how much longer she could endure the looks of sympathy and words of condolence. Every time it felt like she was just moving on from losing her parents and having her entire world turned upside down, someone would remind her of it again.

She didn't need reminding.

More than an hour later, Hannah sat and listened to the deacon's sermon. Today's sermon was about opportunities. The deacon spoke of Gott opening doors and leading you to crossroads. How prayer would allow you to take the right turn.

When the deacon ended the sermon, it was with a verse that made Hannah smile. It not only applied to her current place in life, but it applied to her confusing feelings for Joseph as well.

Esther 4:14 Perhaps this is the moment for which you have been created.

The verse renewed Hannah with hope for the future. It assured her that Gott had a plan for her life and that she had been created to face the challenges that had come her way.

That was why, when the service was over, she couldn't wait to find Joseph. She no longer cared about what was the right way to go about letting him know she liked him as well, instead she wanted to tell him.

Before she could search for Joseph, Isabel found her. They talked about Thanksgiving that was only two weeks away, and Isabel reissued her invitation once again. From the corner of her eye, Hannah saw Daniel approach with Joseph by his side.

Her heart skipped a beat and even if she wanted to, she couldn't stop the smile from forming on her mouth.

Daniel lured Isabel away for a private moment to talk, giving Hannah and Joseph a little privacy.

"It's gut to see you, Hannah," Joseph admitted with a smile.

Hannah nodded. "Jah, it felt strange not to see you this week."

Joseph chuckled. "Did you miss me, Hannah? I thought I was the enemy?"

Hannah shook her head. "You're too nice to be the enemy. Perhaps I missed you… just a little."

Joseph smiled and shuffled nervously in place. Hannah wasn't sure what he was nervous about, but changed the subject. "Everyone is planning for Thanksgiving; do you have any plans?"

Joseph shook his head. "Not yet, but I was hoping you might change that?"

Hannah frowned. "Me?"

Joseph nodded. "Hannah…I'm tired of beating around the bush. I like you. I really like you and I didn't expect to like you at all."

Hannah's heart soared with hope as laughter bubbled from her throat. "That's gut, because… I like you too."

Relief flooded Josephs' features as his smile broadened. "Then would you accept an invitation to join me for Thanksgiving dinner? I usually spend it alone, not wanting to intrude on other families and this year… I know it's going to be hard for you. Let me be there for you."

Hannah glanced at Isabel, who was talking to Daniel, and quickly decided. She knew her friend would understand. "Alright, Joseph. But can you cook?"

Joseph frowned and let out a heavy sigh. "This is where honesty comes in. I can cook… chicken stew and meatloaf."

Hannah laughed when he confirmed her suspicions. "Why don't I change those plans just a little? You come over and I'll cook Thanksgiving dinner."

"Then what do I do?" Joseph asked, pretending to be insulted.

Hannah shrugged with a mysterious smile. "Really? I have to spell it out for you?"

"Jah, because I wanted to make the evening special for you and now you're doing it for me." Joseph seemed a little offended.

Hannah's smile broadened. "You can take me on a buggy ride after dinner. A *real* buggy ride, if you want to?"

When Joseph's eyes brightened with joy and humor at the same time, Hannah couldn't help but laugh. "I didn't realize you were asking me on a buggy ride at the fair."

Joseph chuckled. "I just thought you weren't interested…"

"I was, I mean I am," Hannah laughed shyly.

"Then I look forward to joining you for Thanksgiving supper. Might I be as forward to ask about your stuffing?" Joseph asked hopefully.

Hannah nodded. "I make a pear, pecan, and sausage stuffing. It's the one my mamm taught me. I hope you have nothing against pear stuffing?"

Joseph's mouth practically watered. "Actually, I was hoping for pear stuffing. I had it once at an aunt's haus but she passed away soon after. I've met no one that makes pear stuffing since."

"And then you met me…" Hannah smiled at him with warmth in her eyes. She felt her heart expand with hope. Perhaps this was the moment she had been created for.

Or at least, Thanksgiving was.

She had two weeks to prepare for the most important meal of her entire life. Perhaps this Thanksgiving she would have more to be grateful for than what she had anticipated.

Chapter 24
A Courtship Takes Flight

"Hannah, that was the best turkey I've ever had. If I followed my daed's advice, I might have to ask for your hand right now," Joseph said when he finished his second plate of food.

Hannah laughed, feeling flattered by his compliment. "I'm sure it wasn't that gut. What was your daed's advice?"

"It was that gut," Joseph insisted. "My daed used to say the day I met a woman that could make me smile and bring a smile to my belly, she would be the right one."

"I didn't know a belly could smile," Hannah teased.

Joseph nodded, his eyes remaining serious. "It can, and right now, mine is smiling from rib to rib."

Laughter bubbled from Hannah's throat. She had been nervous about Joseph coming to dinner tonight. In fact, she had been so nervous that she had tossed the first batch of stuffing and made a new one, afraid that the first one was too spicy.

She had braided her hair three times before she felt it was good enough, and she had even dusted the living room twice.

With a fire crackling in the hearth, the house had been warm and inviting when Joseph arrived. It was a cool evening, a clear sign that the first snow would fall in the weeks to come. They had enjoyed a cup of coffee prior to having dinner, and now Hannah couldn't help but feel excited for the buggy ride they were about to go on.

Hannah gathered their empty plates and headed for the kitchen. She wanted to go on the buggy ride with Joseph, but, she couldn't help but fear that it would be freezing out. The wind was howling, the leaves being tugged this way and that as the cold snap moved in.

She didn't hear Joseph's footsteps, but she could feel his presence as he moved into the kitchen.

"Let me at least do the dishes, Hannah. I'm sure you've spent the whole day cooking," Joseph offered.

Hannah shook her head. "Nee, you will not do the dishes. My mamm always said if you invite guests for dinner, they shouldn't have to pay for it by doing the dishes."

Joseph chuckled. "Seems like we were raised by wise people."

"We were," Hannah agreed.

Joseph moved towards her and took both of her hands in his. When he met her gaze, Hannah felt warmth and joy pulse through her veins. When Joseph looked at her like he was doing in that moment, Hannah felt as if her entire world had opened up and that the man by the side of the road that day had quoted the right verse to her.

Joseph was part of Gott's plan to prosper her, she was sure of it. The wind howled loudly, and Hannah shivered at the thought of going for a buggy ride. "Joseph..." she trailed off, not wanting to give him the wrong impression. "Joseph,

I've been looking forward to going on a buggy ride with you for two weeks."

It was the first time Hannah was completely honest with Joseph about her feelings for him. She couldn't help but feel slightly exposed by the honesty. "But right now, this minute, I fear I'm not brave enough to face the cold. Would you mind if we went on a buggy ride another time?"

Joseph searched her gaze for a moment before his mouth curved into a smile. "Do you know why they brought in the tradition of a buggy ride? It's so that two young people could get to know each other in private. So that they could talk without having their families interfere and the whole community gossip about where their courtship was going. We can do that right here in your living room. We can sit by the fire and drink cocoa and learn more about each other. I don't need to take you out in my buggy to spend time with you Hannah, I just want to spend time with you."

Hannah's heart swelled in her chest. "I'd like to sit by the fire and have cocoa with you."

Joseph's eyes narrowed slightly. "There is one condition though…"

"What would that be?" Hannah asked with a frown.

"Our first cup of cocoa by the fire is the beginning of our courtship. Before you even make that cocoa, Hannah, I want you to know that I intend to ask for your hand in marriage before long. You're everything I didn't know I needed, everything I've always wanted. My relationship with your father might have been complicated, but I'm sure if he were here, he would give his blessing knowing that I can provide for you and that I make you happy. I make you happy, don't I?"

Hannah's laughter filled the kitchen. "You do. Now let's find out how much we have in common."

After she had made them cocoa, Hannah and Joseph went to sit by the fire. Hannah hadn't been sure what they would talk about, but soon they were talking about everything and anything. They talked about farming pumpkins, winter chores, family traditions and their hopes for the future.

When Joseph finished his third cup of cocoa, he stood to leave. Hannah wanted him to stay, but she knew their evening had come to an end.

Besides, she had a feeling there would be many more evenings by the fire with Joseph in her future.

She walked him out, but he stopped her on the porch with a firm look. "Don't come out. I don't want you to catch a cold."

"I'll be fine," Hannah insisted.

Joseph smiled at her with love in his gaze. "Part of allowing someone into your life, Hannah, is allowing them to take care of you. Just like I'm telling you to stay inside, I'm telling you I'll be by this week to split wood for the fireplace."

"But… Isabel's daed said he would do it," Hannah quickly argued.

Joseph held up his hand. "Then I just have to do it before he does. Gut night, Hannah, denke for… for being you."

As Hannah watched Joseph climb into his buggy and drive away, her smile broadened.

Plans to prosper her indeed.

Epilogue

"I can't believe it's that time of year again," Hannah admitted to Isabel as she looked at the two giant pumpkins on the scale. One was theirs and the other was from a competing farmer in a different community.

Isabel nodded. "I know. This time last year, you and Joseph were still at war and Daniel was still trying to charm me into accepting his hand in marriage."

"Well, it didn't take him very long, did it? Your wedding was a week after new year's," Hannah teased.

Isabel huffed irritably. "Don't remind me. I just have three more weeks to go. The doctor said it's going to be thanksgiving twins."

"Goodness, that must be exciting." Hannah touched her friend's swollen belly. It overjoyed her that not only had Isabel found a good husband, but all her dreams were about to come true. For as long as Hannah could remember, Isabel had spoken about being a frau and a mamm.

"it's terrifying. I can hardly manage taking care of a calf. How am I going to raise two helpless little babies?" Isabel asked, wide-eyed.

Hannah touched her arm and smiled warmly at her friend. "You'll be just fine. Generations of women have done it and you will do it the same way.

"You're right, it's just... it's overwhelming to know I'm having two at the same time."

"And I'll be there to help," Hannah assured her.

"Joseph is calling you," Isabel gestured to where Joseph was standing with the judges beside their giant pumpkin.

"Excuse me." Hannah moved towards her husband and felt the familiar warmth of joy and love fill her body. She might have teased Isabel about her wedding that had taken place so soon after their courtship had begun, but she and Joseph didn't waste any time either.

Before they had begun to till the dirt on both pumpkin farms, they had celebrated their vows on the bishop's farm. They had filled the day with friends and distant family in the community, although neither Joseph nor Hannah had any close family left.

That day, they had begun their own family.

They had moved into Hannah's house, although they farmed both farms. Isabel and Daniel had moved into the house on Joseph's farm and Daniel now acted as farm manager there.

Together, they had worked the fields side by side. They had grown pumpkins and fallen deeper in love over the summer. It was hard to imagine how overwhelmed Hannah had been the year before, when now she found Joseph turning to her for advice.

With the money she had won from the fall fair, they had fertilized both farms and had enough left to open a savings account to plan for the future. Between their two farms, Hannah knew they had security to build a life together.

A wonderful life.

But then, she turned to him for advice just as often.

The judges had done the measuring and color assessment of the pumpkins that morning and now it was time for final weigh in. She couldn't help but feel a little anxious.

They had sowed Atlantic Giant seeds on both farms, but once again the vines closest to Hannah's home had yielded the biggest fruit. For her and Joseph, it was both evidence that the more love and attention you gave something, the better it grew. They had set out a table and two chairs in the center of their prized vines, and enjoyed their morning coffee there every day during the summer.

"Are you ready for the weights?" Joseph asked when she joined him.

Hannah nodded eagerly. "I am. Do you regret not entering a prize winner from your farm?"

"You mean our other farm? And the answer is no. Prize winners grow best when they get the most attention, they get the most attention while we share our morning kaffe conversation with them."

Hannah smiled. "Gut, then, at least we agree on that."

The judge, the same one as the year before, took the podium. He repeated the same speech from the year before, giving everyone the background of giant pumpkins and explaining that they would donate the pumpkins to charity.

But then he continued with some extra words he had added to his speech. "Last year, we had two competitors in the final. This year, these two have joined forces, and hearts, and have entered only one pumpkin. Before we announce this year's winner, we at the fall fair want to wish Hannah and Joseph all the best of luck with their marriage and we hope to see them at the fair for years to come."

The Amish community clapped and celebrated the personal message before the judge stepped toward the scales. "The time has come for us to choose this year's winner."

Hannah held her breath even as Joseph reached for her hand. When the scales lit up and the weights were revealed, Joseph's cries of delight could be heard from miles away.

Their pumpkin had won the grand prize at the fair by two hundred pounds. It was a win unlike any win before, and once again Hannah had broken her father's record, as well as her own record from the year before.

"This is the best blessing we could've asked for, Hannah," Joseph's voice was brimming with excitement as he turned to her.

Hannah shook her head and shrugged. "Nee, it isn't."

Joseph frowned. "Except for you?"

"Except for this." Hannah's hand rested on her belly as a smile curved her mouth.

Joseph's eyes widened with surprise and joy. "We're expecting a boppli?"

Hannah nodded. "Now we can raise pumpkins and kinner."

When their gazes met, the cheers from the crowd, the prize money, everything, disappeared.

It was just Hannah and Joseph and the family they had found in each other.

*** The End ***

Thank you kindly for choosing to read my book. I sincerely hope you enjoyed it. All of my Amish Romances are wholesome stories suitable for all to enjoy.

If you could be so kind to leave a review on Amazon, I would appreciate it.